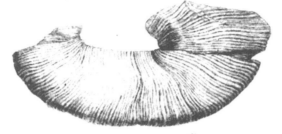

CHARLES DARWIN

The Life of a Revolutionary Thinker

CHARLES DARWIN

The Life of a Revolutionary Thinker

DOROTHY HINSHAW PATENT

Holiday House / New York

In memory of my father, H. Corwin Hinshaw (1902–2000),
who taught me to love science and nature

ILLUSTRATION CREDITS

Charles Darwin's Diary of the Voyage of H.M.S. "Beagle" edited by Nora Barlow.
    Cambridge, England: Cambridge University Press. 1923: 32
Darwin Archives, by permission of the Syndics of Cambridge University Library:
    6, 16, 18, 27, 59, 63, 66, 85, 102, 103, 118, 119, 124, 125, 126
Dorothy Hinshaw Patent: 11, 15, 23, 47 top and bottom, 48, 49, 55, 69, 71,
    77, 79, 111, 116, 121
English Heritage: 10 left, 60, 81
Journal of Researches by Charles Darwin: John Murray, 1890: 56
Journal of Researches by Charles Darwin, T. Nelson, Sons, 1890: 2, 29, 37,
    39 left and right, 40, 42, 43, 46, 50, 52
Dr. Milo Keynes: courtesy of Dr. Milo Keynes: 10 right
National Portrait Gallery, London, courtesy of the National Portrait Gallery, London:
    70, 93 left and right, 96, 109, 110, 114

Endpapers: engraving of fossil shells from *Geological Observations on the Volcanic Islands and Parts of South America Visited during the Voyage of H.M.S. Beagle*

Library of Congress Cataloging-in-Publication Data

Patent, Dorothy Hinshaw.
    Charles Darwin : the life of a revolutionary thinker /
        by Dorothy Hinshaw Patent. — 1st ed.
        p. cm.
    Includes bibliographical references (p. 139).
    ISBN 0-8234-1494-9 (hardcover)
        1. Darwin, Charles, 1809–1882—Juvenile literature.
    2. Naturalists—England—Biography—Juvenile literature.
    [1. Darwin, Charles, 1809–1882. 2. Naturalists.]
    I. Title.
    QH31.D2 P38 2001
    576.8'092—dc21
    [B]   00-037034

CONTENTS

MAN · IS · BVT · A · WORM ·

# PROLOGUE

Have you ever wondered why you keep getting colds or the flu year after year or questioned why finding a genuine cure for AIDS is taking so long?

The answer to these puzzles lies in a process discovered by Charles Darwin in 1838, called natural selection. Before Darwin, most biologists believed that God created every species of living thing on Earth in its final form, perfectly suited to the environment in which it lived. Darwin spent decades gathering evidence from all disciplines of biology that existed in his time, as well as from geology, to demonstrate that species vary and change over time. As Darwin showed, species change in response to conditions in their environments.

His principle explains the tremendous variety of living things on Earth. It also explains many mysteries of nature, such as why you can catch one cold after another. The viruses that cause colds and flu change continually. When you get sick, your body produces chemicals called antibodies that fight off the infection. But these antibodies work only against the strain of virus that infected you. Because they change, different strains of viruses can infect you the next year. You may feel the same symptoms, but you actually have a slightly different disease. Every year, scientists scramble to produce new flu vaccines. They try to figure out what strains of flu will be around the following winter and develop vaccines that can fight those strains.

The vaccines "teach" the body to resist the strains the scientists have chosen. But other strains will survive in their victims and go on to reproduce, be passed on, and make other people sick.

The same principle applies to AIDS. One reason AIDS is so hard to treat is that the AIDS virus keeps changing, or evolving, into different forms. When a new drug comes along, it works for a while, but resistant strains of the disease multiply and spread. They continue to survive and plague us according to Charles Darwin's theory of evolution by natural selection.

But in 1809, the year of Darwin's birth, almost nothing was known about disease. Science was based on the authority of ancient "experts" whose ideas went unchallenged. Experimental science did not exist as an accepted discipline. But Darwin's time was one of great intellectual activity and radical change in how people lived. When he was born, there were also no photographs, no surgical anesthetics, no railroad trains, no telegraphs, and no electricity in homes. By the time he died in 1882, professional photography was well established, patients were blessedly unconscious during surgery, railroads spanned continents, telegraph wires carried messages at lightning speed across the miles, and homes were being wired for electricity.

During Darwin's lifetime, science also changed into a system based on observation and experimentation and became an academic discipline. Darwin's work helped stimulate these changes. His principle of evolution by natural selection gives us the most powerful tool we have in understanding how the living world works. Without it, biology makes no sense. For this reason, writers like John Bowlby can declare, "Charles Darwin . . . is the most influential biologist to have lived. Not only did he change the course of biological science but he changed for ever how philosophers and theologians conceive of man's place in nature."

CHAPTER ONE

The Passion for Collecting

CHARLES ROBERT DARWIN, the fifth child and second son of Susannah Wedgwood Darwin and Robert Waring Darwin, came into the world on February 12, 1809, when his mother was forty-three years old. He was born in the family home, called The Mount, which stood on a hill just outside the town of Shrewsbury, in Shropshire County, in the west of England.

At the time of Charles's birth, the Darwins' other children were Marianne, age ten; Caroline, age eight; Susan, age five; and Erasmus, age four. Fifteen months after Charles's birth came the last child, Catherine. Both the parents came from respected families, established members of the upper middle class who had earned their money through hard work. Josiah Wedgwood I, Charles's maternal grandfather, had established a very successful pottery manufacturing business that is highly regarded to this day. Charles's other grandfather, Erasmus Darwin, had been a famous scientist and poet who died before Charles was born.

Charles grew to be an imaginative boy who loved the outdoors. He enjoyed fishing and exploring the countryside around the family estate. An avid collector, he gathered pebbles and dead insects during his outdoor adventures. At home he hoarded stamps and the wax seals used to close letters. The young Charles meticulously labeled the things he collected. For example, about one old broken bit of tile he wrote: "A piece of tile found in Wenlock

Charles's father, Robert Waring Darwin, and Susanna Wedgwood Darwin, Charles's mother

Abi. C. Darwin, January 23, 1819." As he wrote much later, in his autobiography, "The passion for collecting, which leads a man to be a systematic naturalist, a virtuoso, or a miser, was very strong in me."

Charles and his younger sister, Catherine, spent hours together on the grounds of The Mount. They developed a complex code language they used while playing. While Charles hid in an old tree, Catherine sent him messages on a series of ropes and pulleys.

According to other people, Charles was a pleasant, quiet child. But in his autobiography he wrote that he tried to attract attention through lies and exaggeration:

> I may here also confess that as a little boy I was much given to inventing deliberate falsehoods, and this was always done for the sake of causing excitement. For instance, I once gathered much valuable fruit from my father's trees and hid it in the shrubbery, and then ran in breathless haste to spread the news that I had discovered a hoard of stolen fruit.

His father seemed to be aware of his son's fabrications and paid little attention, so Charles eventually gave up the lies.

Charles's older sister Caroline had the job of teaching him. Caroline was only a teenager, and not the most patient or understanding instructor. Charles wrote:

Before going to school I was educated by my sister Caroline, but I doubt whether this plan answered. I have been told that I was much slower in learning than my younger sister Catherine, and I believe that I was in many ways a naughty boy. Caroline was extremely kind, clever and zealous; but she was too zealous in trying to improve me; for I clearly remember after this long interval of years, saying to myself when about to enter a room where she was "What will she blame me for now?" and I made myself dogged so as not to care what she might say.

The Mount, Charles's childhood home, which today houses government offices

Later in life, Charles devoted several pages of his autobiography to his father. He admired his father's skill as a physician and his character and mental abilities. He literally saw his father as larger than life:

> He was about 6 feet 2 inches in height, with broad shoulders, and very corpulent, so that he was the largest man whom I ever saw. When he last weighed himself, he was 24 stone [336 pounds], but afterwards increased much in weight. His chief mental characteristics were his powers of observation and his sympathy, neither of which have I ever seen exceeded or even equalled.

Charles admired his father when he himself was an adult, but when Charles was growing up Robert Waring Darwin was often away. When he was at home, he monopolized the family's attention. He could be demanding and autocratic. Although he had plenty of money, he didn't like spending it. His wife, Susannah, worked hard to help him and worked as a receptionist for his medical practice.

Most Darwin biographers describe Charles's father as a busy physician and absentee father who believed his son was a poor student destined for mediocrity. However, Janet Browne, a respected scholar trained as both a zoologist and a historian of science, presents a very different picture. In her biography *Charles Darwin Voyaging,* she writes of Charles's father:

> He particularly liked sharing his pleasure in gardening with his son, explaining the names of plants, perhaps reading them out of the botanical textbook composed by a great-uncle of Charles's also named Robert Waring Darwin, or reciting lines from a scientific poem *The Botanical Garden,* published in 1791 by Grandfather Erasmus.

She also writes that Dr. Darwin often took Charles along in his carriage on medical visits and that he gave Charles books from his own library that were precious mementos of his late brother. His brother had died while a medical student, and Dr. Darwin had named Charles after him.

Janet Browne does not believe that Dr. Darwin was an overbearing father, and she feels that he appreciated Charles's interest in natural history. She quotes Charles's sister Caroline writing that their father had "the highest opinion of his [Charles's] understanding & intelligence. My father was very fond of him & even when he was a little boy of 6 or 7, however bustled & overtired, often had C. with him when dressing to teach him some little thing."

However, Charles believed his father thought he was a mediocre fellow who would never make much of himself. This belief affected Charles for his entire life and may have contributed to his later strong need for the approval of his colleagues.

Charles's mother was frequently sick. Her pregnancy with her second child, Caroline, had been difficult, and she never quite recovered from it. She also suffered off and on from headaches and intestinal upsets. Ill health wore down her spirits. In 1816 or 1817, she became chronically ill.

Susannah's health took a sudden turn for the worse in July 1817. No one knows for certain what ailed her, but her symptoms of terrible abdominal pain and vomiting indicate that she probably had either a perforated ulcer or cancer. Her two younger sisters and her two older daughters tended her. She suffered terribly her last few days, finally passing away on July 15 at the age of fifty-two.

The younger children, including eight-year-old Charles, were kept away during the last two weeks of their mother's illness and allowed to see her only one last time after she died. Charles's memories of the event were fragmented. He couldn't remember the illness or the household turmoil that surely surrounded the tragedy. In his autobiography, he recalls only "her deathbed, her black velvet gown, and her curiously constructed work-table." In *The Life of Charles Darwin* his son Francis quotes an earlier memoir that states:

When my mother died I was 8 ½ years old, and [Catherine] one year less, yet she remembers all particulars and events of each day whilst I scarcely recollect anything . . . except being sent for, the memory of going into her room, my father meeting me—crying afterwards.

As an adult, Charles could not recall much else about his mother, either—just a walk or two together and her comment that if she asked him to do something, it was for his own good.

Historians of biology do not agree on the impact of Susannah's death on her younger son. Some believe it a pivotal event that explains Charles's ill health in later years. Others think that his relationship with his mother was less important than those with his loving sisters and servants, such as the devoted nanny, Nancy.

CHAPTER TWO

A True Schoolboy

IN THE SPRING OF 1817, several months before his mother's death, Charles and Catherine had begun attending a local day school run by Reverend Case of the Unitarian chapel. The Wedgwoods, Charles's mother's family, belonged to the liberal Unitarian Church instead of the more conservative state church, the Church of England. This was unusual for the time, but Susannah followed her family's tradition. Susannah also attended Case's chapel on Sundays with the children. Later, however, Charles was confirmed in the Church of England.

Charles studied at Reverend Case's school until the age of nine, when he was sent across town to Shrewsbury School, what is called in Britain a "public" school. In Britain, a public school is actually a private boarding school, and the sons of gentlemen were usually sent to such schools when quite young. Charles's brother, Erasmus, had already been studying there for a few years. In public schools the older boys had authority over the younger ones. Academic learning at these schools was considered less important than learning about life. As quoted in *Boys Together* by John Chandos, one English gentleman wrote to another:

> I grant the system of education is bad—that a boy learns little and there are many objections to a public school—but it fits a boy to be a man—to know his fellow creatures—to love them—to be able to contend with the difficul-

Shrewsbury School, today the town library

ties of life—to attach friends to him—to take part in public affairs—to get rid of his humours and caprices & to form his temper and manners—to make himself loved and respected in the world. . . .

In Darwin's time, a proper education focused on classical Greek and Roman literature. Samuel Butler, the headmaster at Shrewsbury School, believed passionately in this system. He was convinced that "the country owes all that is tasteful and elegant in literature" to the classics. When Butler became headmaster in 1798, the school's reputation had declined. By 1818, when Charles began his studies there, the school had become highly respected due to Butler's efforts.

Life at the school was difficult for Charles. A long dormitory with a single window at one end housed up to thirty boys. During the night, boys used chamber pots kept under their beds instead of toilets. Sixty years later, Charles could still remember the stench, saying that just the thought of the "atrocious smell of that room in the morning" still nauseated him. Nights were cold and dank, and Charles got Erasmus to complain to their father, who took the matter to Butler. The headmaster refused to give the boys more blankets, claiming that all the boys would then expect them, at an increased cost to their parents.

Physical punishment was acceptable practice, even for poor grades, and Dr. Butler was known for his fondness for the rod. As quoted in *Shrewsbury School Register, 1734–1908,* edited by J. E. Auden, he objected to his reputation, claiming, "I have never flogged the same boy twice [in] a week more than three times in twenty-six years."

Shrewsbury School lay less than a mile from The Mount, and young Charles frequently ran home during the day to visit his family, often barely making it back to school in time for nighttime lockup. Being torn from his family less than a year after his mother's death must have been very difficult for Charles, but he made the best of the situation. Although a quiet boy, he made friends easily with boys both older and younger than himself.

Charles and his younger sister Catherine, drawn in 1816

Later in life, Charles commented that Shrewsbury School provided him "the great advantage of living the life of a true schoolboy." However, it contributed nothing to his education. Charles wrote of the school:

Nothing could have been worse for the development of my mind than Dr. Butler's school, as it was strictly classical, nothing else being taught, except a little ancient geography and history.

Bored in school, Charles also found it hard to learn Latin and Greek. Later he commented, "During my whole life I have been singularly incapable of mastering any language." At the same time, his intellectual curiosity led him to continue "collecting minerals with much zeal, but quite unscientifically—all that I cared about was a new-named mineral, and I hardly attempted to classify them." He also observed insects and birds closely and wondered in his boyish enthusiasm "why every gentleman did not become an ornithologist."

Away from the classroom, Charles also enjoyed reading Shakespeare's historical plays and a book called *Wonders of the World*, which he believed "first gave me a wish to travel in remote countries."

In their teens, Charles and Erasmus carried out chemistry experiments in the tool house at The Mount, earning Charles the nickname "Gas" at school. The two boys often worked late into the night. "This was the best part of my education at school, for it showed me practically the meaning of experimental science," he later wrote of the experience.

Charles may have valued this scientific endeavor, but science was not considered a proper study for a budding country gentleman. "I was also once publicly rebuked by the head-master, Dr. Butler, for thus wasting my time on such useless subjects. . . ."

During Charles's residence at Shrewsbury School, guns became very popular with the students. Dr. Butler had a big problem on his hands, with boys bringing knives and loaded guns to school. Disaster was barely averted on several occasions. In June 1820, there was a confrontation between two groups of students hostile to one another. Today we would probably call them gangs. At least one group carried loaded pistols.

Such turmoil must have been both exciting and frightening to the younger boys in the school, like Charles. Perhaps this fascination with weapons at the school contributed to Charles's own fondness for firearms. "How well I remember killing my first snipe, and my excitement was so great that I had much difficulty in reloading my gun from the trembling of my hands," he wrote.

Country gentlemen in Charles's time grew up learning to shoot. They spent many hours on their estates riding and hunting. These activities partly defined an English gentleman, and many men conversed about little else. As he grew up, Charles spent a great deal of his free time hunting with his uncle Josiah Wedgwood II on the Wedgwood estate, Maer Hall. Josiah's own four sons were not outdoor types. Josiah valued Charles's companionship greatly, and included him whenever possible on sporting weekends during the partridge and pheasant seasons.

Dr. Darwin saw no value in Charles's preoccupation with the natural world and with chemistry. What mattered to him was success in academic studies. In 1825, Dr. Darwin removed Charles from Shrewsbury School two years early.

Only a few occupations were considered suitable for the sons of gentlemen. Charles's poor performance in the classics meant he could never become a lawyer, so continuing in the family tradition of medicine seemed to make sense. Erasmus was following this course. He needed to spend a year study-

Charles's brother, Erasmus, at age 15

ing at a certified medical school before he could practice medicine. He would be going to Edinburgh University in Scotland. Their father decided that Charles should join Erasmus in the fall. Charles could attend medical lectures and, when he was old enough, formally carry on his studies. The plan pleased both boys, who looked forward to being together. They made plans to continue their chemical experiments and go on expeditions to collect fossils.

Although Charles was only sixteen years old, he spent that summer helping his father make medical calls to the poor of Shropshire. Dr. Darwin even assigned some women and children to Charles as patients. Charles wrote down their symptoms, and his father advised him about what medicines to dispense. Charles enjoyed the work, and it looked as though he had found his vocation.

Arriving in Edinburgh in late October 1825, the boys found rooms only a few minutes' walk from the university. The brothers thought Edinburgh an exciting city, but Charles was soon once again bored by his classes:

> The instruction at Edinburgh was altogether by lectures, and these were intolerably dull, with the exception of those on chemistry.... Dr. Munro made his lectures on human anatomy as dull as he was himself, and the subject disgusted me.

Many years later, Charles wished he'd been encouraged to practice dissection. He was sure it would have changed his attitude toward anatomy and been of use in his future scientific endeavors. For Charles, book learning and boring lectures always seemed remote from what mattered. He wanted to experience things himself, not read or hear about them from others.

Charles, however, was too sensitive to practice medicine. Visiting wards full of sick people distressed him. At that time, no anesthetics were available, and patients suffered terrible pain as their bodies were cut into. He wrote later:

> I also attended on two occasions the operating theatre in the hospital at Edinburgh, and saw two very bad operations, one on a child, but I rushed away before they were completed. Nor did I ever attend again, for hardly any inducement would have been strong enough to make me do so; this being long before the blessed days of chloroform. The two cases fairly haunted me for many a long year.

The violence and agony of surgery, combined with the dull classroom lectures, convinced Charles that medicine was not for him.

Besides, Charles didn't care about completing his medical studies. He had figured out that his father was sufficiently wealthy that he would never have to work for a living. In a letter to his sister Susan, from Edinburgh, January 29, 1826, his lack of concern is obvious:

I have been most shockingly idle, actually reading two novels at once. A good scolding would do me a vast deal of good. I hope you will send one of your most severe ones.

His attitude was not lost on his father. On March 27, Susan wrote:

My reason for writing so soon is, that I have a message from Papa to give you, which I am afraid you won't like; he desires me to say that he thinks your plan of picking & chusing what lectures you like to attend, not at all a good one; and as you cannot have enough information to know what may be of use to you, it is quite necessary for you to bear with a good deal of stupid & dry work: but if you do not discontinue your present indulgent way, your course of study will be utterly useless.—Papa was sorry to hear that you thought of coming home before the course of Lectures were finished, but hopes you will not do so.

Despite his disillusionment, Charles entered into a second year of study at Edinburgh. He pursued independent study of natural history, including learning how to stuff birds. Erasmus had left to continue his studies in London, and now Charles made friends with other young men interested in natural science. They went on collecting jaunts to the shore, gathering up tide pool creatures and accompanying fishermen trawling for oysters. Students interested in natural science belonged to a group called the Plinian Society, which met at the university to read and discuss scientific papers. Charles also belonged to the Royal Medical Society and attended its meetings.

Robert Grant, an unconventional educator trained as a doctor in Edinburgh, strongly influenced Charles during his second year at the medical school. Grant joined Charles on outings to gather invertebrate specimens to dissect. Grant pioneered scientific observation of sponges, studying their structure and development, and coining their scientific name, *Porifera*. Working with Grant, Charles experienced the joy of scientific discovery, of being the first person to observe a natural phenomenon and describe it for posterity. Charles's first scientific paper, which he presented at the Plinian Society in 1827, was the result of his work with Grant. Grant admired the evolutionary ideas of the French naturalist Jean Baptiste Lamarck and Charles's grandfather Erasmus. Charles wrote much later in his autobiography:

> He one day, when we were walking together burst forth in high admiration of Lamarck and his view on evolution. I listened in silent astonishment, and as far as I can judge, without any effect on my mind. I had previously read the *Zoonomia* of my grandfather, in which similar views are maintained, but without producing any effect on me. Nevertheless it is probable that the hearing rather early in life such views maintained and praised may have favored my upholding them under a different form in my *Origin of Species.*

After two years of medical school, Charles was absolutely certain he did not want to become a doctor. His father worried about his apparently aimless son: "You care for nothing but shooting, dogs, and rat-catching, and you will be a disgrace to yourself and all your family," he yelled at Charles. He knew that there must be a profession suitable for this wayward son. He suggested joining the clergy. After all, Charles liked natural history, and tramping about in the countryside noting the marvels of nature was considered a fine hobby for a country parson. Charles asked for time to think about it. He liked the idea, but he wasn't sure he agreed with all the dogmas of the Church of England.

After reading several books on the doctrines of the church, Charles decided he could feel comfortable taking on religious studies: "[A]s I did not then in the least doubt the strict and literal truth of every word in the Bible, I soon persuaded myself that our Creed must be fully accepted."

So it was decided. Charles would go to Christ's College, Cambridge, where Erasmus had taken his undergraduate studies, to begin his course for the clergy. But before he could begin, he needed tutoring. He had forgotten almost everything he had learned of the classics, and he would need Greek and Latin. Through the fall of 1827, Charles studied with a private tutor. At the end of Christmas vacation, he was off to Cambridge.

CHAPTER THREE

Cambridge

ONLY MALE MEMBERS of the Church of England could attend the colleges of Cambridge. Although united under the Cambridge name, each college had its own faculty. Like the faculty and other students, Charles had to wear a cap and gown as he strode around the ancient university. The faculty's gowns differed depending on the degrees they had received, and undergraduates and graduates did not wear the same gowns and caps. Sons of noblemen wore tasseled caps in some colleges, as well as distinctive gowns to distinguish them from more ordinary students like Charles. Erasmus advised his brother to always wear his cap and gown and to follow the other Cambridge rules as well.

The rules were many. Students had to attend chapel every morning at eight o'clock. They then met with their tutors, who were Cambridge graduates called fellows. Fellows had a permanent role in governing the university, and they were not allowed to marry. Lectures by professors were given in the afternoons. After dinner at five in the dining hall, the undergraduates had some free time, but they had to be back to their college by nine.

Charles fit in well at Cambridge. Most of the students came from similar backgrounds and were studying with the same goals. He made many friends and enjoyed various recreational activities. Once again, however, he proved ill-suited to formal studies.

Christ's College, Cambridge University, where Charles studied for his Bachelor's degree

Although . . . there were some redeeming features in my life at Cambridge, my time was sadly wasted there and worse than wasted. From my passion for shooting and for hunting, and, when this failed, for riding across country, I got into a sporting set, including some dissipated low-minded young men. . . .

Charles downplayed the serious side of his time at Cambridge. Perhaps he enjoyed it so much he didn't think of it as serious. He got to know his cousin William Darwin Fox, who was in his last year and also studying for the clergy. The two hit it off immediately. Fox was also an avid collector. His college rooms were graced by a motley array of specimens ranging from huge stuffed swans to moth pupae.

Insects, especially beetles, were Fox's specialty, and Charles joined his cousin in pursuing these fascinating and varied insects. In the process, he learned how to collect systematically and identify specimens precisely. Even during the summer holidays, when the young men went home to their families, Charles couldn't let up. "I am dying by inches from not having anybody to talk to about insects," he complained to Fox in a letter from June 1828. He went on to describe some beetles he had found and to beg Fox to write back.

Charles was so determined to collect unusual specimens that sometimes he ran into trouble:

> One day on tearing off some old bark, I saw two rare beetles and seized one in each hand; then I saw a third and new kind, which I could not bear to lose, so that I popped the one that I held in my right hand into my mouth. Alas it ejected some intensely acrid fluid, which burnt my tongue so that I was forced to spit the beetle out, which was lost, as well as the third one.

Since Charles was studying for the clergy, science courses weren't required, but Fox also encouraged Charles to join him in studying botany with John Stevens Henslow, a young professor with progressive ideas. Only after Fox left did Charles sign up with Henslow, who gave Charles the only formal science training he received at Cambridge.

Charles took to Henslow immediately. His lively lectures focused on plants as vital living things, not dry, dusty museum specimens. Field trips were integral to Henslow's teaching methods. During these jaunts into the country, Henslow paused now and then to talk about the rocks or animals they encountered along the way as well as the plants, for he was a knowledgeable naturalist.

Charles frequently attended Friday evening gatherings at Henslow's home where ten to fifteen guests sipped tea, observed curiosities of nature, and discussed science. Henslow became Charles's mentor. Charles joined the Henslow family for meals and accompanied the professor on long walks in the country so often that he became known as "the man who walks with Henslow." Charles wrote affectionately of his mentor in his autobiography:

His knowledge was great in botany, entomology, chemistry, mineralogy, and geology. His strongest taste was to draw conclusions from long-continued minute observations. His judgement was excellent, and his whole mind well-balanced. . . . His moral qualities were in every way admirable.

During the holidays, Charles studied hard. He had decided not to go for honors, as the honors exam covered only mathematics and classics. After taking the regular examination for a BA degree on January 22, Charles was pleased to find he scored 10th out of the 178 nonhonors candidates.

Charles decided to take a break from his studies. While at Cambridge, Charles read Alexander von Humboldt's account of his adventures in the jungles of South America from 1799 to 1804. Humboldt wrote vividly of the beauty of the rain forest and the magnificence of the Andes and conjured up scientific theories based on his observations of nature. Charles yearned to follow in Humboldt's footsteps, to be an explorer and a naturalist. He decided that once his studies ended, he would organize a small expedition to Tenerife, one of the Canary Islands, which Humboldt had visited on his way to South America.

In April 1831, Charles wrote to Fox, "I talk, think, & dream of a scheme I have almost hatched of going to the Canary Islands. —I have long had a wish of seeing Tropical scenery & vegetation: & according to Humboldt Teneriff is a very pretty specimen."

The trip ran into a critical hitch: when Charles inquired about passage and fares in July, he discovered that passenger ships left for the islands only in June. He would have to wait another year.

Meanwhile, Henslow convinced Charles that he needed to learn something about geology to get the most from his adventure. The volcanic nature of Tenerife had fascinated Humboldt. Henslow, who had taught mineralogy before turning to botany, began to instruct Charles.

The perfect opportunity for studying geology, however, came when Henslow asked Adam Sedgwick, a dynamic young Cambridge geology professor, to take Charles along as an assistant during his summer research trip to north Wales. The two tramped across the country for a week. Sedgwick taught Darwin all along the way, showing him fossils and explaining how to interpret geological history. Charles also learned how to make accurate field drawings and maps.

Charles thought this information would be useful during his short Tenerife adventure. In the meanwhile, he contemplated finishing his theological studies and then settling down as a country parson, the way William Darwin Fox had done, once he returned from the Canary Islands.

All Charles's plans, however, changed when he received a letter in late August 1831 from Henslow:

> I shall hope to see you shortly fully expecting that you will eagerly catch at the offer which is likely to be made you of a trip to Terra del Fuego & home by the East Indies—I have been asked by Peacock who will read & forward this to you from London to recommend him a naturalist as companion to Capt Fitzroy employed by Government to survey the S. extremity of America. . . .

Charles jumped at this unique opportunity and decided to accept. His father, however, had other ideas. The trip would be dangerous; the ship, called the *Beagle,* cramped and dirty; and the entire venture a deviation from Charles's chosen career as a cleric. Charles wrote Peacock and Henslow, reluctantly turning down the offer. But Dr. Darwin gave Charles one small hope when he told his son, "If you can find any man of common sense who advises you to go, I will give my consent."

Charles knew just the man to consult, his uncle Josiah Wedgwood II. Charles knew his father might be persuaded to change his mind if his respected brother-in-law found merit in the venture.

Charles carefully drew up a list of his father's objections and presented it to his uncle. Josiah could see how badly Charles wanted to go, and he realized that such a trip was the dream of a lifetime for an adventurous young man like his nephew. He wrote back to Robert Darwin, meeting his objections one by one, ending by pointing out that "looking upon him [Charles] as a man of enlarged curiosity, it affords him such an opportunity of seeing men and things as happens to few." Convinced, Charles's father withdrew his objections, and Charles immediately wrote Henslow and Peacock saying he would accept after all.

The Darwin family threw itself into a frenzy preparing for the voyage. Dr. Darwin provided money, since Charles was expected to cover all his expenses and pay for his equipment. Charles's sisters rounded up his wardrobe and

10

(1) Disreputable to my character as a Clergyman hereafter

(2) A wild scheme

(3) That they must have offered to many others before me, the place of Naturalist

(4) And from its not being accepted there must be some serious objection to the vessel or expedition

(5) That I should never settle down to a steady life hereafter

(6) That my accomodations would be. most uncomfortable

(7) That you should consider it as again changing my profession

(8) That it would be a useless undertaking

Charles's list of his father's objections to accepting the position on the Beagle

labeled his shirts for the laundry, and Charles consulted with Henslow and others about supplies. There was no time to lose, as the *Beagle* was to depart as early as September 25, less than four weeks away. All that remained was for Charles to meet Captain FitzRoy and receive his approval.

CHAPTER FOUR

A Shore-Going Fellow

THE PURPOSE OF THE *Beagle*'s voyage was to survey and chart the oceans, especially along the South American coastline. This would be its second trip to do so. The nineteenth century was a great time for exploration for western European countries. Spain and England in particular had colonies and commercial interests in South America and around the world. In those days, all ships were powered by the wind. When the wind wasn't blowing, they were helpless victims of ocean currents, which could drive ships onto the rocks or ground them in shallow waters. Knowing the offshore depths in areas where ships traveled near coastlines was critical to successful navigation, and thus to successful commerce.

The first *Beagle* trip lasted more than four years, from May 22, 1826, to October 14, 1830. During this voyage, another, larger ship, the *Adventure*, accompanied the *Beagle.* The two ships were charged with surveying the southeastern coast of South America, then around the dangerous and stormy island off the southern tip called Tierra del Fuego and finally up the western side as far as the island of Chiloé, in Chile. The southwestern side of South America consists of a maze of islands, peninsulas, and inlets, a nightmare for surveying ships that had to rely on the wind to get them where they wanted to go.

The difficulties of surveying Tierra del Fuego drove the *Beagle*'s mentally unstable captain, Pringle Stokes, to suicide at the end of May 1828, and

Artist's rendition of the Beagle, *1890*

Robert FitzRoy was appointed the new captain of the *Beagle.* The survey was continued, but not completed.

In 1831, FitzRoy was reappointed to command the second surveying voyage that would complete the survey and then continue around the world from the west coast of South America. The *Beagle* was to make a complete series of measurements at regular intervals around the globe called meridians. Such information would make navigation across the vast oceans much more accurate.

Longitude can be determined only if the time is known exactly, so FitzRoy brought along twenty-two very precise clocks called chronometers, whose accuracy he checked regularly.

On September 5, 1831, Charles and FitzRoy met, and they got along well. FitzRoy, however, wanted to be sure Darwin understood the circumstances of the voyage. He warned Darwin that the food would be plain and the ship crowded. The *Beagle* might not continue around the world, he said, and if Charles at any point decided he didn't want to continue, he could be let off in "some healthy, safe & nice country" until he could catch a ship back home.

That evening they met for dinner, after which Charles wrote a euphoric letter to John Stevens Henslow:

> Gloria in excelsis is the most moderate beginning I can think of.—Things are more prosperous than I should have thought possible.—Cap. Fitzroy is every thing that is delightful, if I was to praise half so much as I feel inclined, you would say it was absurd, only once seeing him. . . .
>
> You cannot imagine anything more pleasant, kind & open than Cap. Fitzroys manners were to me.

FitzRoy had ordered a drastic remodeling of the *Beagle.* He raised the deck by twelve inches in the forward section and eight inches in the aft. This increased the headroom below decks and made the accommodations much more pleasant for the crew. He also installed some innovative features such as a new, safer type of stove and lightning conductors that protected the ship during electrical storms.

Since the *Beagle* was a vessel of the British navy, it was outfitted as a warship, even though its mission involved surveying, not fighting. The navy thought two guns would be enough, but FitzRoy, a perfectionist, wanted nine. He insisted on brass rather than iron so they wouldn't interfere with his compasses.

As a surveying vessel, the *Beagle* had to carry several small boats to be used for taking measurements: two whale boats, each twenty-eight feet long, two other relatively large boats, and a smaller dinghy.

The remodeling was taking longer than anticipated, and departure was rescheduled for October 10. In the meantime, Charles dashed about London, gathering equipment and supplies: bottles for preserving specimens, a rain gauge, a rifle and two pairs of pistols, a telescope, a compass, and other items.

On September 11, FitzRoy took Charles to Devonport to see the *Beagle* for the first time. In a letter to his sister Susan, Charles seemed taken aback by the diminutive size of the vessel and of his accommodations. "The vessel is a very small one. . . . The want of room is very bad, but we must make the best of it. . . ."

Delays continued. Finally, Charles arrived in Plymouth late in October, excited about the prospect of departing soon: "What a glorious day the 4th of November will be to me—My second life will then commence, and it shall be as a birthday for the rest of my life," he wrote to FitzRoy.

Unfortunately, with so many extensive changes to be made, the ship was still far from ready for departure, and Charles couldn't even begin to stow his gear because his shared cabin was not completed. He wrote to Henslow: "Our Cabines are fitted most luxuriously with nothing except Mahogany: in short, every thing is going on as well possible. I only wish they were a little faster.— I am afraid we shall not bona fide sail till 20th next Month."

The refitted *Beagle* had two relatively large cabins. FitzRoy's cabin, where Charles ate, contained a bed, a couch, a small writing desk, and a small table with two seats, one for FitzRoy and one for Charles at mealtimes. The largest cabin was built on top of the rear deck and called the poop cabin. It served several functions, even though it was no more than eleven feet square. One of the ship's masts stuck right up through the cabin, which housed the ship's library, a washstand, a chest of drawers, and an instrument cabinet. A large table took up the center of the room, and during the day, the cabin functioned as the ship's chart room. Charles also used it as his worktable.

At night, this cabin was Charles's sleeping quarters, which he shared with Midshipman Philip Gidley King, the fourteen-year-old son of Philip Parker King, commander of the *Beagle*'s first expedition. The two young men slung their hammocks on either side of the cabin. Space was at a premium: "The corner of the cabin," Charles wrote to Henslow, "which is my private property, is most wofully small.—I have just room to turn round & that is all."

Cramped though Charles's quarters were, his cabin was spacious by comparison to the accommodations of most on board. The *Beagle* carried sixty-seven people, a very large number for a ninety-foot-long ship. The artist, Augustus Earle, had a cabin barely big enough for a bed, six feet long by five feet wide.

Finally, Charles was able to move on board the *Beagle* on December 3, 1831, expecting to depart the following Monday. He had been constantly busy since September, acquiring everything he needed for the voyage, then finding a way to fit it into the small space allotted to him. Despite the delays, his sense of humor remained undampened as can be seen in this diary entry:

> I am writing this for the first time on board, it is now about one o'clock and I intend sleeping in my hammock. I did so last night and experienced a most ludicrous difficulty in getting into it; my great fault of jockeyship was in trying to put my legs in first. The hammock being suspended, I thus only succeeded in pushing [it] away without making any progress in inserting my own body.

Still, the wait was hard on Charles. After stowing away his things, he had plenty of time to worry about whether he'd made the right choice. He would be away from his family and friends for years, among a completely different kind of men. He was a landsman who felt completely out of place on board a ship. But he resolved to seize the opportunity. He wrote an agenda for himself in his diary on December 13:

> The principal objects are 1st, collecting, observing & reading in all branches of Natural history that I possibly can manage. Observations in Meteorology, French & Spanish, Mathematics, & a little Classics . . . If I have not energy enough to make myself steadily industrious during the voyage, how great & uncommon an opportunity of improving myself shall I throw away. May this

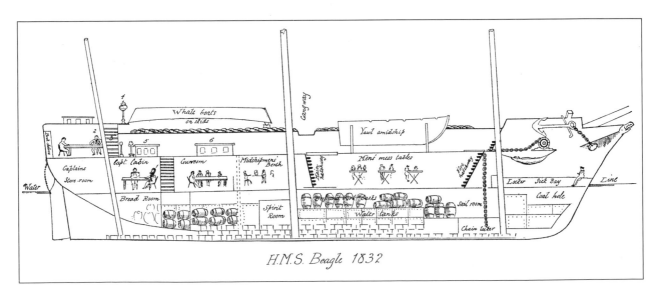

Diagram of the Beagle *by Phillip Gidley King*

never for one moment escape my mind & then perhaps I may have the same opportunity of drilling my mind that I threw away whilst at Cambridge.

Life on board the *Beagle* was a new experience for Charles. Discipline on vessels of the Royal Navy was severe and the rules were many. Even before leaving port, he tasted the less pleasant side of naval life. Throughout Christmas day, the sailors drank and partied wildly to celebrate the holiday. The next day, Charles wrote:

A beautiful day, & an excellent one for sailing, the opportunity has been lost owing to the drunkedness & absence of nearly the whole crew. The ship has been all day in a state of anarchy. . . . Several [sailors] have paid the penalty for insolence, by sitting for eight or nine hours in heavy chains.

Many of the sailors also received a flogging, their bare backs being struck by a cat-o'-nine-tails. This whip had a short wooden handle to which lengths of knotted cord were attached. Flogging, said one observer, "made a bad man worse, and broke a good man's heart."

When the *Beagle* finally departed on December 29, 1831, any sense of anticipation was dampened by the seasickness Charles described in his diary: "[T]he misery is excessive and far exceeds what a person would suppose who had never been at sea more than a few days."

The next day things were, if anything, worse: ". . . wretchedly out of spirits and very sick. I often said before starting, that I had no doubt I should frequently repent of the whole undertaking, little did I think with what fervour I should do so."

FitzRoy thought Charles would give up and leave the ship at the first scheduled stop, Tenerife in the Canary Islands, the place Charles had wanted so badly to explore after reading Humboldt's exotic narrative. But the officials at Tenerife feared that British sailors might carry the cholera that was plaguing several British cities and would not let them off the ship.

The disappointed Charles wrote in his diary: "Oh misery, misery . . . we have left perhaps one of the most interesting places in the world, just at the moment when we were near enough for every object to create, without satisfying, our utmost curiosity."

Charles got a break from his seasickness when the *Beagle* made landfall in mid-January 1832, at St. Jago, one of the Cape Verde Islands about 450 miles off the west coast of Africa. From the sea, the volcanic island looked like a black, austere landscape. But inland, in the valleys, Charles could finally explore the tropical paradise he had dreamed of for so many months. He wasn't disappointed:

> Here I first saw the glory of tropical vegetation. Tamarinds, Bananas & Palms were flourishing at my feet. . . . I returned to the shore, treading on Volcanic rocks, hearing the notes of unknown birds, seeing new insects fluttering about still newer flowers.—It has been for me a glorious day, like giving to a blind man eyes.

The plant and animal life weren't the only joys of the island. Its geology was fascinating as well. Charles was intrigued by the island's geography. Lying forty-five feet above the water in a cliff was a white stratum of calcium carbonate with shells embedded in it. It was sandwiched between two layers of volcanic rock.

Once this land had been under the sea. Now it stood forty-five feet above the water. What caused it to rise? At the time, scientists believed that the geological features of Earth came about through rapid, violent activities in the recent past. But the newly published first volume of Charles Lyell's *Principles of Geology* postulated a completely different scenario. Lyell believed that the same forces that shaped the planet today had altered it in the past, a past that he believed extended millions of years, not merely the few thousand years that most geologists thought.

Charles had been reading Lyell, and the white layer in the rock made him think. One of Lyell's ideas was that land can rise up or sink down slowly and maintain its basic structure. The white layer wasn't fractured and angled as if it had been violently elevated. Charles could only explain what he saw through Lyell's explanation. He saw that corals and oysters under the sea had been covered by molten lava, forming a layer that turned white over time. Then the layer had been gradually elevated to its present position.

Charles was excited. It was only the first stop of the voyage, and his mind was already full of new and exciting thoughts. He began to think of himself as a scientist, as someone who could make real contributions to the understanding of the natural world.

While Charles explored the island, the *Beagle* crew took measurements. This became a pattern for the entire voyage—Charles would explore the land while the ship carried out its duties. As a matter of fact, Charles spent far more time ashore than he did on board. The voyage lasted almost five years, yet Charles endured just 533 days (about eighteen months) at sea. For as long as four months at a stretch, he traveled on land, usually on horseback.

This arrangement delighted Charles, for he never got used to being at sea and suffered from seasickness throughout the voyage. "I loathe, I abhor the sea and all ships which sail on it," he wrote to his sister Susan. To William Darwin Fox he complained, "I hate every wave of the ocean with a fervour, which you who have only seen the green waters of the shore can never understand."

Charles took advantage of every opportunity to collect specimens, whether on land or aboard the *Beagle.* He brought along gear for gathering fish and invertebrate animals that lived in the open ocean as well as tide pool plants and animals and those that lived on land.

Charles worked hard when the ocean was calm enough to keep his stomach under control. He wrote in his diary and scientific notebooks, observed specimens under his microscope, prepared specimens, made drawings, and wrote letters. Despite his seasickness, he came to enjoy the peace and quiet and orderliness of shipboard life during calm seas. Early in the voyage he wrote to his father: "I find to my great surprise that a ship is singularly comfortable for all sorts of work.—Everything is so close at hand, & being cramped, makes one so methodical, that in the end I have been a gainer."

On shore, he spent every possible moment collecting specimens and observing natural phenomena. During much of the voyage, Darwin focused on geology. He became expert at reading the geological clues he encountered, and these supported Lyell's theories. Even if he hadn't come up with the theory of the origin of species by natural selection, Darwin would be remembered as an important geologist.

After surveying around St. Jago, the *Beagle* began the long journey across the Atlantic Ocean. The ship stopped briefly at St. Paul's Rocks, a cluster of tiny islands where great numbers of seabirds nested. Then the *Beagle* reached the equator, halfway between the North and South Poles.

Crossing the equator is traditionally accompanied by much ritual and merriment. Charles and the other first-timers were locked below decks and brought up one by one. Charles was the first victim. Blindfolded, he was brought on deck, roughly shaved, and decorated with pitch and paint, then dunked in a large vat of water. He got off relatively easily, however, as the dining companion of the captain; others had "dirty mixtures" put in their mouths and rubbed on their faces.

The night of the nineteenth of January, the ship anchored off the island of Fernando Noronha, where they stayed only long enough for FitzRoy to check the accuracy of his chronometers. From there, they crossed the expanse of the Atlantic Ocean and arrived at Bahia, Brazil, on February 28, 1832.

While Charles always treasured his first experience of the tropics at St. Jago, he reveled even more in his first view of the Brazilian rain forest, writing in his diary on February 29:

> The day has passed delightfully. Delight itself, however, is a weak term to express the feelings of a naturalist who, for the first time, has been wandering by himself in a Brazilian forest. . . . To a person fond of natural history, such a day as this, brings with it a deeper pleasure than he even can hope again to experience.

The horrors of slavery soon prevented Darwin from enjoying the pleasures of nature. Slave ships from Africa arrived in Brazil, and Darwin was shocked by the treatment of blacks. Both of his grandfathers had been leaders in the British antislavery movement, so Charles was already sensitive to the issue. But nothing is more impressive than personal experience, and the degradation of the Brazilian slaves that Charles witnessed appalled him.

His strong objections to the slave trade almost ended his stint on the *Beagle.* He and FitzRoy argued bitterly about the subject. FitzRoy didn't support slavery, but believed slaves were better off than free but dirt-poor people. After all, he told Charles, he had heard slaves reply when asked by their owners that they did not want to be free. Charles expressed doubts about this answer and FitzRoy blew up. How dare Darwin question his word; Darwin would now have to leave the ship.

Charles was stunned. The officers invited him to dine with them and explained FitzRoy's terrible temper. When he cooled off, they said, he would see his error. Sure enough, FitzRoy soon apologized and invited Darwin to return to his dining table. The two men avoided the subject of slavery from then on.

The Brazilian forest, portrayed in 1890

From Bahia, the *Beagle* sailed on to Rio de Janeiro, then the capital of Brazil. Charles described their arrival to Caroline:

We lay to during last night, as the Captain was determined we should see the harbor of Rio & be ourselves seen in broad daylight.—The view is magnificent. . . . Mountains as rugged as those of Wales, clothed in an evergreen vegetation, & the tops ornamented by the light form of the Palm.—The city, gaudy with its towers & Cathedrals is situated at the base of these hills, & command a vast bay, studded with men of war the flags of which bespeak every nation.

Charles received mail from home in Rio. Eagerly, he opened and read letters from his sisters Caroline and Catherine, his cousin Charlotte Wedgwood, and his colleague Henslow. "England is gone mad with marrying, you will think," wrote Catherine. Indeed both Charlotte and Fanny Owen, a young woman whom Charles had hoped he might court and marry upon returning from the voyage, were now engaged. Charles realized that by the time he returned to England, his world would have changed considerably.

CHAPTER FIVE

South American Adventures

WHILE THE *BEAGLE* TOOK measurements along the coast, Charles and the ship's artist, Augustus Earle, rented a cottage on Botafogo Bay, near Rio, until June 27, 1832. Charles adventured inland, visiting ranches where he saw more of the evils of slavery. At Botafogo, he explored forest and shore, continually marveling at the beauty and diversity of the tropics.

He focused mainly on small creatures, discovering many spiders new to science and uncovering flatworms that lived on land. When he wrote to Henslow about the land-dwelling flatworms, the older scientist replied skeptically. All flatworms known to science lived in water, so Darwin must have found unusual slugs, he reasoned. Henslow's reaction only made Charles more determined, and he looked for flatworms throughout the voyage. He was learning to trust his own observations.

As the *Beagle* continued south along the South American coast, the landscape changed from lush forest to the seemingly endless grasslands of the Argentinean pampas. Charles spent as much time ashore as possible, riding over the pampas, observing the unfamiliar wildlife, and helping hunt for meat to feed the crew.

One September day, while sailing along the Argentinean coast in one of the small boats, Darwin and FitzRoy came across a massive deposit of shells and bones. Here were fossils of huge ancient animals. Charles could hardly wait until the next day, when he returned with a crew of sailors to help dig up the remains.

He conveyed his excitement in a letter to Caroline written on October 24, 1832: "I have been wonderfully lucky, with fossil bones.—some of the animals must have been of great dimensions: I am almost sure that many of them are quite new."

Charles knew he had found something sensational. A giant head of an extinct creature dug out of the soft rock became one of the most important finds of the entire voyage. The only fossils of giant mammals from South America in England were the remains of a single ground sloth, and here was the skull from another. Along with the other bones, the skull was shipped off to Henslow. Altogether, Darwin had found parts of at least six animals. Besides the ground sloth, the fossils also included parts of a giant extinct armadillo and a hooved animal the size of a rhinoceros. By the time Charles returned home, his reputation as an explorer and naturalist was already firmly established, largely because of these spectacular fossils.

On the *Beagle*'s return trip to Buenos Aires, Argentina, in October, a mar-

Darwin found fossil bones of these two extinct animals in South America,
a megatherium (left) and giant ground sloth (right).

The port of Buenos Aires during the 1800s

velous nighttime display of bioluminescence enchanted Darwin, who wrote in *The Voyage of the Beagle:*

> The vessel drove before her bows two billows of liquid phosphorus, & in her wake was a milky train.—As far as the eye reached, the crest of every wave was bright; & from the reflected light, the sky just above the horizon was not so utterly dark as the rest of the heavens.

Today, we know that the display came from tiny single-celled creatures in the water called dinoflagellates.

In late November, the ship stocked up in Montevideo for the long and dangerous trip through the waters around Tierra del Fuego. In the mail at Montevideo, Charles received the second volume of Lyell's *Principles of Geology.* In this volume, Lyell had to deal with a key element of Christian dogma in the early nineteenth century, the immutability of species. It stated that God had created the species, each and every one separately, making each exquisitely adapted to its environment. Uncovering God's glorious creation constituted a major goal of naturalists who explored the far reaches of the planet, observing and collecting ever more beautiful and amazing plants and animals. Ultimately, it was this entrenched belief that Darwin later challenged, first in *The Origin of Species* and then in *The Descent of Man* and other works.

By the time he arrived in Montevideo, Charles had become a firm advocate of Lyell's geology. But in his second volume, Lyell shrank from the biological implications of his geological theories. He could not bring himself to extend his own logic and suggest that species, like landscapes, could change over time. Instead, Lyell proposed that species became extinct one by one as geological changes modified the environment. Then, he believed, each species was replaced by a newly created one that was better adapted to the altered environment. Reading Lyell's second volume probably helped keep Charles convinced of the prevailing opinions he would have to maintain if he were to become a country parson. But later on, his own discoveries would force Charles to make a break with Lyell's biological theories.

When the *Beagle* departed from Montevideo on December 4, everyone was reminded that during the vessel's first trip, Captain Stokes had been driven to suicide by the stresses of surveying the stormy, wild region they were approaching.

Tierra del Fuego harbored indigenous people unused to Europeans, as well as unpredictable waters. On the previous voyage, FitzRoy had taken four native Fuegians captive and brought them to England. One had died there, but the others had been converted to Christianity and adopted European ways. They were now being returned to their native soil, along with an English missionary named Richard Matthews. FitzRoy hoped that Matthews, with the help of the three now "civilized" Fuegians, would be able to "tame" the natives, teaching them how to farm and making good Christians out of them.

When the *Beagle* entered the Bay of Good Success on Tierra del Fuego, a group of Fuegians hailed them. The next morning, FitzRoy sent out a party, including Darwin, to meet with the indigenous people.

Despite his amazement at the wildness of these people, Charles could still appreciate their talents:

They are excellent mimics: as often as we coughed or yawned, or made any odd motion, they immediately imitated us. . . . They could repeat with perfect correctness, each word in any sentence we addressed them, and they remembered such words for some time. Yet we Europeans all know how difficult it is to distinguish apart the sounds in a foreign language. Which of us, for instance, could follow an American Indian through a sentence of more than three words?

A group of Fuegians in front of their home, 1890

Late in life, when Charles contemplated the place of mankind in nature, he would remember the Fuegians.

The *Beagle* crew settled Matthews and the three English-educated Fuegians at a locale called Woolya, setting up temporary housing, unloading the items brought along for their use, and helping plant a garden. The experiment eventually failed, however, and Matthews gave up his plan of "civilizing" the natives and returned to England.

Charles spent most of the rest of 1833 on land. He traveled on board in March to East Falkland Island, where he received an important letter from Henslow. Darwin had been sending his specimens to Henslow at every opportunity, but until he read this letter, he had no idea whether they had arrived in good condition and whether Henslow believed them to be worthwhile. Henslow wrote: "I think you have done wonders. . . ." The letter relieved Charles greatly and gave him renewed confidence.

At the end of April 1833, Charles moved into the town of Maldonado along the coast of Uruguay. He enjoyed adventuring with the local cowboys, called gauchos, and collected huge numbers of specimens—eighty species of birds within the distance of a morning's walk from his house, as well as mammals and snakes.

A gaucho using bolas to hunt, 1890

All these specimens had to be examined (Charles noted what foods were in their stomachs and other details), then skinned. He couldn't do the work alone, so he enlisted the aid of the ship's fiddler and odd-job man, sixteen-year-old Syms Covington. Covington was already a good shot and learned how to skin specimens quickly. In July, FitzRoy agreed to let Charles hire Covington as his full-time servant. Covington became vital to Darwin's research and stayed with him until Charles married in 1839.

The *Beagle* finally left the tip of South America, after taking endless measurements around the tortuous coastline and abundant islands. As the *Beagle* worked her way up the west coast of South America, Charles again explored on land whenever possible. A major trip inland in August 1834 allowed him to check out the geology at the base of the Andes. On January 19, 1835, he saw his first volcanic eruption. The *Beagle* lay safely offshore, surveying the island of Chiloé, when Mt. Osorno on the mainland erupted during the night. Charles was seeing the powerful forces of geology in action.

More impressive than the volcano, however, was the violent earthquake that followed four weeks later. Charles wrote in *The Voyage of the Beagle*:

FEBRUARY 20TH—The day has been memorable in the annals of Valdivia, for the most severe earthquake experienced by the oldest inhabitant. I happened to be on shore, and was lying down in the wood to rest myself. It came on suddenly, and lasted two minutes; but the time appeared much longer. . . .

A bad earthquake at once destroys the oldest associations: the world, the very emblem of all that is solid, has moved beneath our feet like a crust over a fluid; one second of time has conveyed to the mind a strange idea of insecurity, which hours of reflection would never have created.

Soon Charles saw the dramatic consequences of the quake. Not only were towns and villages destroyed, the land became visibly elevated, just as Lyell had written. Now that Charles had witnessed such an event personally, he could see that over vast stretches of time, a series of elevations could create mountains as dramatic as the Andes. Then, from March 18 to April 10, Charles crossed the Andes, where he could see the evidence of past elevations of the land as he traveled higher and higher into the mountains. In *The Voyage of the Beagle,* he wrote of how he reveled at the new experience.

The short breathing from the rarefied atmosphere is called by the Chilenos 'puna.' . . . The only sensation I felt was a slight tightness over the head and chest; a feeling which may be experienced by leaving a warm room and running violently on a frosty day. There was much fancy even in this; for upon finding fossil shells on the highest ridge, I entirely forgot the puna in my delight. . . . The inhabitants all recommend onions for the puna . . . for my part, I found nothing so good as the fossil shells!

 CHAPTER SIX

The Galapagos and Beyond

ARWIN'S VISIT TO THE Galapagos has inspired scientists and writers ever since the publication of *The Origin of Species.* The popular image shows Charles observing Galapagos wildlife, especially the birds, then being inspired by the realization that they had developed through the evolutionary process he discovered, called natural selection. This scenario is completely incorrect.

In fact, Charles arrived at the islands thinking of himself primarily as a geologist. He looked forward to analyzing the volcanic landscape more than the living things. In the first edition of *The Voyage of the Beagle,* finished early in 1837 but published in 1839, Charles wrote mostly about the geology, the tortoises, and the iguanas of the islands. The birds are merely listed with brief descriptions.

The unique life on the islands, especially the mockingbirds and the finches, did get Charles thinking that species might not be immutable but rather had changed over time. However, that realization came only after his return to England, after the ornithologist John Gould had examined Darwin's specimens and given his conclusions.

The Galapagos Islands, the *Beagle's* first stop on the trip across the Pacific Ocean, lie about six hundred miles off the coast of Ecuador, straddling the equator. In Darwin's time, these harsh but beautiful islands provided a haven for whaling vessels, which anchored in their harbors to gather water and food, largely in the form of the then abundant giant tortoises. The tortoises could survive for weeks on board a ship without eating or drinking and provided an important source of fresh meat for sailors.

The Galapagos Islands consist of ten major islands of varying size and many smaller ones. The *Beagle* navigated around all but one of the larger islands, but Charles only spent time on shore at four. The first landfall for Charles came at what the British labeled Chatham Island, which today is called by its Spanish name, San Cristobal. In his narrative of the voyage, FitzRoy wrote: "We landed upon black, dismal-looking heaps of broken lava, forming a shore fit for pandemonium. Innumerable crabs and hideous iguanas started in every direction as we scrambled from rock to rock. Few animals are uglier than these iguanas. . . ."

Darwin was just as unimpressed. He wrote in his diary:

The black lava rocks on the beach are frequented by large (2–3 ft.) most disgusting, clumsy lizards. . . . Somebody calls them 'imps of darkness.' They assuredly well become the land they inhabit. When on shore I proceeded to botanize and obtained ten different flowers; but such insignificant, ugly little flowers, as would better become an arctic than a tropical country.

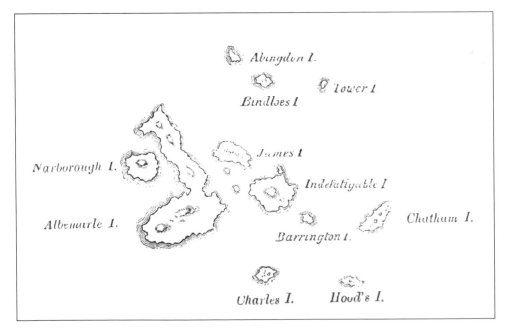

A map of the Galapagos *from the* Voyage of the Beagle, *using the British names for the islands, 1890*

Above: Much of the Galapagos Islands still consists of black lava. Here, a marine iguana and a lava lizard rest on the lava on Fernandina Island

Right: A land iguana, which evolved from the same ancestor as the marine iguana, on Plaza Island

Everyone was amazed at how tame the animals were. Charles pushed a hawk off a branch with the end of his gun, and Midshipman King killed a finch with his hat. After exploring the shore and bringing eighteen tortoises on board, the *Beagle* anchored for the night. The next day, Charles and Covington went on shore for an overnight stay, observing the volcanic landscape and collecting plants, birds, shells, and insects.

The next stop was Charles Island (now called Floreana), upon which a penal settlement had been built. While the lowlands were dry, the highlands, where the settlement was located, were quite green and lush. During Charles's visit, the vice-governor of the islands said he could tell just by looking at a tortoise's shell which island it came from. Unfortunately, Darwin believed the tortoises were imports from the Indian Ocean, transplanted by pirates as a food source. If they weren't native wildlife, he had decided he had no need to collect specimens, so the idea that the tortoises varied didn't catch his interest. Darwin did, however, notice that the mockingbirds here differed significantly from those on Chatham Island (now called San Cristobal), so he collected and labeled them. Later, these birds would figure prominently in his ideas of evolution.

A young Galapagos tortoise feeds on a blossom on Isabela Island

On September 28, the *Beagle* anchored at Albemarle Island (now known as Isabela), the largest by far of the Galapagos. Isabela, shaped like a backward L, features four major volcanoes. The search for water became more important than for specimens; Charles noted that the few pitiful pits in the rock that held water attracted doves and finches, but he didn't collect these birds. We know today that several species of finches live on Isabela; Darwin thought the finches, unlike the mockingbirds, were similar on all the islands.

Charles spent the most time on James Island (which is now called Santiago). He, the ship's surgeon, Mr. Bynoe, and three other men were dropped off for a week with tents and supplies while the *Beagle* went off in search of water. On Santiago, there were many tortoises. However, the ones living there had shells similar to those on San Cristobal, so Charles concluded that the differences among the tortoises had been overstated. In his diary, he commented on how difficult it was to find a spot to pitch the tents, since the burrows of the land iguanas so disturbed the earth. Sadly, land iguanas are completely extinct on Santiago today.

James Island, where Darwin spent the most time ashore in the Galapagos (This photo was taken from a hill just above where Darwin camped)

During his entire stay on the Galapagos, Charles paid little attention to the finches. Although their beaks were differently shaped, they all seemed like rather small, undistinguished birds to Charles. The males were usually black and the females brown. He collected finches from three islands but didn't label them by island. Later on, this carelessness would haunt him. He also collected birds he identified as blackbirds, a wren, and grosbeaks. However, these, too, were actually finches. Charles was not aware of what he had found until after he returned to England.

The *Beagle* departed from the Galapagos on October 20 to begin the 3,200-mile passage to Tahiti. Charles had almost four weeks to sort out his specimens, read about the South Seas, and contemplate the new islands of swaying palms and beautiful Polynesian women that he would encounter. They arrived on November 15. Tahiti didn't disappoint him, and on November 26, the *Beagle* weighed anchor and sailed for New Zealand.

The three-week passage covered rough seas, and poor Charles again suffered badly from seasickness. As he wrote in *The Voyage of the Beagle*, the passage seemed interminable.

The palace of the queen at Papiete, Tahiti, 1890

It is necessary to sail over this great sea to understand its immensity. Moving quickly onwards for weeks together we meet with nothing, but the same blue, profoundly deep, ocean. Even within the archipelagoes, the islands are mere specks, and far distant one from the other.

After almost four years, Charles was finally heading home. He began to miss his family and friends more intensely. He wrote to his sister Caroline:

For the last year, I have been wishing to return & have uttered my wishes in no gentle murmurs; But now I feel inclined to keep up one steady deep growl from morning to night.—I count & recount every stage in the journey homewards & an hour lost is reckoned of more consequence, than a week formerly.

Charles's comments on New Zealand and Australia in *The Voyage of the Beagle* have mainly to do with the people. His scientific fervor and zeal for collecting may have become exhausted. Besides, in New South Wales, the part of the Australian mainland he visited, native wild animals had already become scarce because of humans and the animals they brought with them. But even in Tasmania, which was far less civilized, Darwin focused more on people than on wild things, writing home about concerts, dinners, and dancing parties, entertainments he had missed for the last few years.

Besides continuing to take meridian measurements, the crew of the *Beagle* had one additional task during the long trip across the Pacific: to investigate coral reefs. Out in the middle of the ocean, a coral reef could be a dangerous obstacle, one that could sink a ship. Lyell had a theory about the formation of reefs, and FitzRoy planned to investigate the Keeling Islands, now called the Cocos, in the Indian Ocean with Lyell's theory in mind. He also needed to take measurements there.

During the voyage, Charles had been puzzling over coral reefs and their origin. He couldn't agree with Lyell's idea that they formed around the rims of submerged volcanic craters. The diameter of some circular reefs measured more than thirty miles, which indicated a huge crater. Charles knew there must be another explanation.

Charles applied his South American research to the reef problem and developed a hypothesis that tied the formation of reefs into Lyell's theory of elevations and subsidences of land. If land rose in some places to form conti-

Whitsunday Island, a coral reef in the Pacific Ocean, 1890

nental mountains, he reasoned, it must sink somewhere else. What would be more likely to sink than the ocean floor?

The tiny polyps that make up the living part of coral can live only in warm, shallow water. So, if coral began to grow around the submerged slopes of a volcanic oceanic island that was gradually sinking, a circular reef would slowly build as the sinking coral died and new polyps grew on top. As long as the top of the undersea mountain remained above the water, the reef would encircle an island. Once the top sank under the sea and disappeared, only a circular reef surrounding a lagoon would be left. Barrier reefs along the shores of continents could also form as the sea floor underneath sank.

From April 1 to 12, 1836, Charles was able to verify his theory about reef formation by studying the Cocos Islands. He waded from one small island to the next, sampling corals and taking measurements. Everything he found supported his hypothesis. Charles had begun to think for himself; he no longer automatically accepted the word of others, even those of someone whom he respected greatly, like Lyell.

As the *Beagle* finally headed for home, Charles began to think about his future. During the voyage, he had become a committed naturalist. He no longer saw himself as a country parson, living comfortably in some out-of-the-way village, preaching on Sundays and enjoying walks through the countryside. Now he looked forward to joining the ranks of professional geologists and continuing his scientific career.

Way back in 1833, while in South America, he had already hinted that science beckoned him in a letter to his sister Catherine:

> I trust & believe, that the time spent in this voyage, if thrown away for all other respects, will produce its full worth in Nat: History: And it appears to me, the doing what *little* one can to encrease the general stock of knowledge is as respectable an object of life, as one can in any liklehood pursue.

On the trip home, Charles was relieved to hear from his sister Susan that the family was coming to accept the idea that Charles probably would not be joining the clergy: "Papa & we often cogitate over the fire what you will do when you return, as I fear there are but small hopes of your still going into the church: —I think you must turn professor at Cambridge. . . ."

Meanwhile, Henslow had been preparing the scientific establishment for Charles's return. He put together a natural-history paper from Charles's letters and read it before the Cambridge Philosophical Society in November 1835. The most important Cambridge scientists attended. Henslow also got some of Charles's notes published and convinced Sedgwick to read Darwin's work before the Geological Society. Lyell served as president at the time and was delighted to find Charles confirming his theory of elevation and subsidence and could hardly wait to meet him. Sedgwick was so impressed that he called on Charles's father and told him his son was a promising scientist.

Everyone aboard the *Beagle* looked forward to returning finally to England. The ship stopped at Mauritius, rounded Madagascar, and stopped at the Cape of Good Hope, then sailed on to St. Helena and the Ascension Islands. It seemed they would soon be home. But the *Beagle*'s arrival in England was delayed more than two weeks because FitzRoy, always the perfectionist, insisted on returning to Brazil to make one final measurement linking the series of meridian distances. Finally, the ship headed for home and arrived in Falmouth on October 2, 1836. Charles took the first available coach and arrived at The Mount on October 5, delighted to be reunited with his family. He had left home just over five years earlier to move aboard the *Beagle*. Now twenty-seven years old, he returned an entirely transformed man.

CHAPTER SEVEN

Becoming a Naturalist

LIKE CHARLES, ENGLAND HAD CHANGED dramatically in five years. At home, his father had become tremendously fat and his health had declined. He had almost stopped practicing medicine. Three of Charles's sisters remained single and still lived at home, but his oldest sister, Marianne, had married a physician who had taken over most of Dr. Darwin's practice. Erasmus now lived on his own in London.

Charles made The Mount his headquarters until mid-December. He dashed about, alternating visits to family with trips to London, where he met Charles Lyell and was elected a fellow of the Geological Society, and to Cambridge, where he visited with Henslow. The rushing around exhausted him, and he finally rented a house in Cambridge to escape the hubbub and settled down with Syms Covington to organize the enormous amount of material he had gathered while on the *Beagle*. He needed to deposit his specimens with qualified scientists who had enough spare time to examine and classify them in a timely fashion. After many inquiries, Charles lined up a dozen experts to study his finds. The fossils, for example, went to Richard Owen, a young scientist on his way to becoming a great anatomist, and the birds to well-known ornithologist John Gould, who had scientifically examined and described birds from around the world.

Turning his journals into a book describing his adventures and some of his scientific discoveries took up much of Darwin's time. FitzRoy had asked

After spending time at The Mount, Charles stayed in this house in Cambridge for a few months before moving to London

Charles for a volume on natural history that would accompany his own official account of both the *Beagle*'s voyages. Writing the book now popularly called *The Voyage of the Beagle* gave Charles an opportunity to reflect on his last five years, to figure out which events stood out as most important, and to determine how the trip had affected his scientific outlook.

From January to September 1837, Charles labored over the book, struggling to condense almost five years of adventure and scientific discovery into a single volume. Meanwhile, the experts carefully examined and described his specimens. Charles didn't know it, but some of the results he was about to get back from his colleagues would change his ideas profoundly.

The bombshell that finally convinced Charles that species are not, after all, immutable, came from John Gould's analysis of the Galapagos birds. After moving to London in March 1837, Charles met with Gould, who informed Charles that all but one of the twenty-six Galapagos land birds he had collected were new to science. He also told him that the mockingbirds comprised three separate species, all different from any found on the continent of South America. A similar species, however, did live on the mainland in Ecuador.

The biggest surprises, however, came from the finches. Charles had thought these birds represented four different subfamilies. Gould, however, recognized that Darwin's blackbirds, his warblers, his wren, and his two different groups of finches were all actually closely related finches. Their nearest relative, Gould told Charles, lived on the northwestern coast of South America.

Why would different species of finches and mockingbirds inhabit nearby islands that offered very similar environmental conditions? Would God have created so many different species just for islands? It made no sense. Lyell's idea that new species were created when conditions changed didn't answer these questions. The islands had virtually the same conditions, yet the species differed.

Transmutation of species—one species changing into others—was the only concept that made sense. Transmutation also explained the existence of mainland relatives and clarified how finches could come to resemble orioles, blackbirds, and wrens. Birds from the mainland, Charles realized, had arrived

Here are four of Darwin's finches, showing their different beaks

on the islands and encountered environments different from the mainland. Over time, they had changed to adapt to those new environments, and they had become new species.

Owen's findings provided Charles with another key piece of information. Charles's fossils, Owen decided, were almost all remains of giant creatures similar to smaller ones that lived in South America in modern times. Charles saw the parallel between the birds and the fossils. The birds had evolved into different forms because they were separated in *space* and could not interbreed. The fossils' descendants had changed over *time* to become something quite different. Given enough miles or years, species in one geographical area could change in significant ways. The Galapagos birds showed that species had changed when separated by space; the fossils showed that species had changed when separated by time. Charles became a convinced evolutionist. A few months later, he began putting his thoughts on paper.

The concept of evolution had been around for a long time. In ancient Greek times, a number of theorists had believed that life developed gradually, from simpler to more complex organisms. But as western civilization developed and Christianity spread, the church's authority replaced the free application of ideas to questions of science. By 1600, the literal interpretation of the Book of Genesis, which states that God created each and every species, had become the orthodox Christian teaching. To say that species might be created in any other way was heresy.

While the concept of the immutability of species reigned through the centuries, a number of biologists had proposed various versions of evolution before the publication of *The Origin of Species.* One person who championed evolution and publicly defied the church was Charles's own grandfather, Erasmus Darwin. Like his grandson, Erasmus Darwin used the differences in domesticated animals to bolster the idea that species could be changed. In his great four-volume work, *Zoonomia; or, the Laws of Organic Life,* published in 1774, he laid out his evolutionary beliefs.

Erasmus wrote that male animals have developed special structures such as antlers to compete for females: "The final cause of this contest amongst the males seems to be, that the strongest and most active animal should propagate the species, which should thence become improved." He pointed out how birds' beaks differ depending on their diet: "All which seem to have been gradually produced during many generations by the perpetual endeavour of the creatures to supply the want of food." Finally, he examined how animals are adapted to protect themselves from predators. Erasmus carefully credited "The Great First Cause" (God) with the origin of life, but he clearly stated his belief that life began as simple forms and changed over "millions of ages" to become the creatures of his time.

Another proponent of evolution, the Frenchman J. B. Lamarck, used many of the same arguments as Erasmus Darwin. Writing between 1800 and 1820, Lamarck developed his theory in greater detail than Erasmus Darwin. Lamarck believed acquired characteristics could be inherited. Thus, if a giraffe stretched its neck longer by straining to reach high leaves, Lamarck said its offspring would inherit the longer neck. He also had other ideas of which biologists disapproved. Thanks to Lamarck, the idea of evolution obtained an aura of scientific unrespectability that lasted until after Charles Darwin published *The Origin of Species* in 1859.

As Charles scribbled in his new notebooks (by October 1838, he had begun his fourth notebook on transmutation), he busied himself becoming firmly established in the scientific community. He served as an honorable secretary of the Geological Society and visited frequently with Lyell. Within two years of his return, he had published six scientific papers based on his *Beagle* discoveries. In 1838, the descriptions of the fossils, birds, and mammals from the voyage began to appear in print. Darwin had become an important and respected naturalist.

In July 1838, he visited his father at The Mount. As Charles had no substantial source of income from his work, his father had continued to support him since his return. Charles needed to know if that support would continue. The two men discussed Charles's future, and Dr. Darwin, who was probably relieved as well as proud that his son had finally found his true path, reassured Charles that his inheritance was ample enough to support him comfortably.

Now that he knew he needn't worry about money, Charles began to consider marriage. Part of him wanted the comfort and security of marriage, but another part worried that a settled life might take time away from his scientific pursuits. He listed the pros and cons of bachelorhood versus marriage. Remaining a bachelor clearly lost out, and Charles began to court his first cousin, Emma Wedgwood, whom he had known since childhood.

In November 1838, Charles proposed to Emma and she accepted. They were married in January 1839 and leased a house in London near the Lyells

Charles made a list of the pros and cons of marrying

and Emma's brother Hensleigh and his wife. The house had plenty of room, with servants' quarters in the attic and spare bedrooms for guests and future children.

From the beginning, Emma, a devout Christian, knew that Charles was more freethinking about religion than she was. She wrote to him before the wedding: "There is only one subject in the world that ever gives me a moment's uneasiness . . . and I do hope that though our opinions may not agree upon all points of religion we may sympathize a good deal in our *feelings* on the subject."

A few weeks after the marriage, she penned another letter dealing with the subject: "May not the habit in scientific pursuits of believing nothing till it is proved, influence your mind too much in other things which cannot be proved in the same way, and which if true are likely to be above our comprehension."

Marriage didn't slow Charles in developing his career. In May 1839, the

Emma Wedgwood
Darwin in 1840

three volumes on the *Beagle*'s adventures and findings were finally published; FitzRoy had taken a long time finishing the first two volumes. Charles's contribution became immediately popular, and on August 15, it was issued as a separate book with the unwieldy title *Journal of the Researches into the Geology and Natural History of the Various Countries Visited by H.M.S. "Beagle."* The book made Charles famous. It received very positive reviews and stimulated the imagination of countless Victorian armchair travelers.

Fame, however, mattered less to Charles than the opinions of those he admired. With some apprehension, he sent a copy to Alexander von Humboldt, who first inspired Charles to want to travel to faraway places. He nervously awaited the great explorer's opinion. The reply could not have been better. Humboldt recognized Charles as an important contributor to science and praised the book itself, predicting "an excellent future" for the grandson of Erasmus Darwin. Charles was thrilled.

CHAPTER EIGHT

The Species Question

A FEW DAYS BEFORE his wedding, Charles was elected a fellow of the Royal Society, making him one of an elite group of only eight hundred scientists worldwide. A week after the wedding, he presented a paper at the Society. His position as a prominent scientist was secure. But no one realized that he was working on an idea that would eventually make him much more than that.

Charles kept his controversial beliefs to himself as he worked on them. He realized that his new ideas would be unacceptable to both science and society. But he continued to develop his theory. He knew that species change, but how? He needed a mechanism.

Charles approached the species problem by collecting every bit of information he could find that might possibly relate to it. He filled notebooks with such entries as "Each species changes. does it progress." and "The tree of life should perhaps be called the coral of life, base of branches dead; so that passages cannot be seen." He also recorded facts like "Rhinoceros peculiar to Java, & another to Sumatra" and "Native dog not found in V. Diemen's land [Tasmania]."

At the same time he wrote in his species notebooks, he kept two other series of notebooks, one on geology and the other on metaphysical questions. His mind raced with ideas stimulated by the long voyage; he wanted to know the answers to so many questions, about both nature and humankind. His strong belief that everything is connected, that humans are a part of nature, is evident in his notes. The pages from the metaphysical notebooks are peppered with references to plants, insects, and dogs, such as "With respect to free will, seeing a puppy playing cannot doubt that they have free will, if so all animals., then an oyster has & a polype (& a plant in some senses, perhaps. . . ."

Despite all his thinking and note taking, one big question remained for Charles. What drove species to change when they reached new territory or encountered new conditions? Since genetics was a completely unknown realm, Charles worked under what could have been a crippling lack of basic knowledge of how traits passed from one generation to the next. During Charles's lifetime, an Austrian monk named Gregor Mendel would conduct experiments with plants that would uncover the basic laws of genetics. His work, however, remained hidden away in an obscure journal until the early twentieth century.

So Charles had only observation to work with. Clearly, offspring resembled their parents in some ways, so at least some traits were passed on from one generation to the next. But what caused changes in those traits?

Fifteen months after he began his first notebook on the transmutation of species in October 1838, Charles came to a great realization:

> I happened to read for amusement Malthus on *population,* and being well prepared to appreciate the struggle for existence which everywhere goes on from long-continued observation of the habits of animals and plants, it at once struck me that under these circumstances favourable variations would tend to be preserved, and unfavourable ones to be destroyed. The result of this would be the formation of new species. Here, then, I had at last got a theory by which to work. . . .

The book Charles referred to, *An Essay on the Principle of Population*, by Thomas Robert Malthus, first appeared in 1798. It dealt with the growth of human populations. He pointed out that most couples at the time had many more than two children and that human populations should thus increase rapidly. Over time, people should outstrip their food supply. However, that did not seem to happen. Therefore, there were clearly checks on population growth such as war, famine, and disease.

Charles knew that species in nature also produce many more offspring

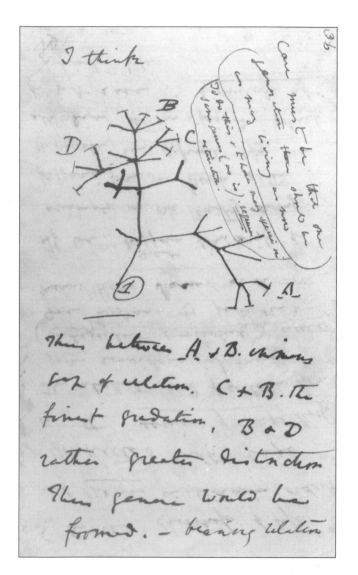

Charles's first sketch of branching evolution in one of his early notebooks

than can survive to adulthood. Reading Malthus made him realize that many individual plants and animals also died before they could reproduce. Those that survived must be better adapted to their environment than those that did not. If the environment changed, the traits of the survivors would be different in some ways from those of earlier generations. Over time, as the differences were preserved, species would change. Finally, Charles had his mechanism, which he called natural selection.

Still, Charles wanted to be sure. He did not want to restrict his research or his thinking and miss other important considerations. So only after over three and a half more years of work that backed up his theory did he allow himself to put his ideas on paper.

During the years between reading Malthus and writing down the first outline of his theory, Charles continued his hunt for facts that would support and explain his ideas or that would contradict them. He read more of Lamarck and his grandfather's great *Zoonomia,* as well as books by other scientists on instinct, reproduction, philosophy, botany, zoology, glaciers, population, chemistry, Australian animals, and anything that might relate to his own ideas.

Whenever he read a scientific paper or a book, Charles made detailed notes. He spent many hours each day reading and summarizing not only books but also articles in the many newly founded scientific journals.

Charles also collected information about domesticated animals. He asked his cousin William Darwin Fox, now living on a country estate, all sorts of questions. He realized that the people most intimately involved with plants and animals, such as zookeepers, farmers, pigeon fanciers, and gardeners, had unique information. When possible, he queried these people in person.

He also began using a new scientific technique. In spring 1839, he sent out a questionnaire with twenty-one detailed questions on animal breeding to farmers he knew. Most of the questions were long and had many parts, but a few, such as "Where *very* different breeds of the same species are crossed, does the progeny generally take after the father or mother?" were relatively simple. Although he received only two replies, they were the beginnings of Charles's studies of domesticated animals that would eventually contribute greatly to the opening arguments in *The Origin of Species.* Questionnaires also gave him a way to get information from far-flung sources, and he would use them again and again over the years.

All the frantic activity of his personal and scientific life began to take a toll on Charles in 1838. From the beginning, Charles realized his controversial scientific ideas would challenge society and religion. During the early nineteenth century, the idea that all species had been separately created by God was Church of England dogma. Archbishop Usher, in the early seventeenth century, had used the Bible to calculate the actual date of the Creation and pegged it at 4004 BC. At that time, he believed, all species had been created, and none had changed since. This idea became the established belief and was included in some editions of the King James Bible.

The fossils uncovered by naturalists during the 1800s, however, forced people to modify this concept. The earliest fossils consisted of simpler organisms. Advanced animals such as birds and mammals appeared only in younger rocks. Therefore, species had to have come into existence at different times in the Earth's history. Despite this new information, the church and scientific community alike still insisted that species do not change. The fossil finds, however, forced a new version of this belief onto scientists—that when conditions changed, old species died out and God created new ones adapted to the new conditions to take their place. According to this theory, the new species God created to replace ones that became extinct were inherently better than the old ones. Thus reptiles were thought to be "better" than fish, and mammals "better" than reptiles. The final result of this constant progress, the theory went, was the greatest species of all, humankind.

Charles worried about the consequences of revealing his theory to the world. He worried about the effects publication of his ideas might have on the Darwin and Wedgwood families and on his scientific reputation. Would he be reviled as an atheist and worse, a fool?

He suffered from heart palpitations and headaches, and his stomach also rebelled. He wrote to his sister Caroline, "The noodle & the stomach are antagonist powers. What thought has to do with digesting roast beef—I cannot say, but they are brother faculties." He visited doctors, who told him he must "knock off work" or he would suffer a breakdown. Charles ignored them.

He had far too much to do to give in to his body. He continued to read voraciously, rereading his grandfather's *Zoonomia* and carefully going through Lamarck's most thorough work, *Philosophie zoölogique,* to make sure that his own ideas were new and different. He also kept up his journals, taking note of his thoughts and ideas and collecting bits of information. Everywhere he went, a notebook went with him, carefully tucked in a pocket in case an idea popped into his head. Meanwhile, the experts examining his specimens sent in more results, and he collaborated with his colleagues in writing up their findings.

Early in 1839, Emma became pregnant. Throughout the year, Charles complained about his health. That summer, they visited his family at Shrewsbury and hers at Maer Hall. Afterward, Charles wrote, "During my visit to Maer, read a little, was much unwell, and scandalously idle. I have derived this much good that *nothing* is so intolerable than idleness."

He was worried about Emma's pregnancy, too, writing to Fox in October, "Emma is only moderately well and I fear what you said is true, 'she won't be better till she is worse.' We are living a life of extreme quietness." Childbirth in those days could be a risky business. Charles's sister Caroline had recently lost a baby a few weeks after birth, giving Charles plenty to brood about.

Finally, on December 24, Charles's health fell apart. He could barely do any scientific work during the next eighteen months. In addition to his previous symptoms, he began to vomit periodically, a problem that would plague him for many years. Meanwhile, on December 27, the baby, named William, was born.

In February 1840, Charles wrote to Lyell, "Is it not mortifying it is now nine weeks, since I have done a whole day's work, & not more than four half days." Things began to improve during the summer, when Charles visited his father, but it didn't last. He took ill again on August 4 and didn't even write letters for five months. Meanwhile, Emma had become pregnant again.

In January 1841, Charles wrote to Fox: "My strength is gradually, with a

Charles with his first child, William, in 1842

good many oscillations, increasing; so that I have been able to work for an hour or two several days in the week. I am forced to live, however, very quietly and am able to see scarcely anybody and cannot even talk long with my nearest relations."

Charles and Emma's daughter, Annie, was born on March 2. Charles's health improved over the next months but was still unreliable. In July, while he visited Shrewsbury and Emma stayed with her family, Charles wrote to her, "I was pretty brisk at first, but about four became bad and shivery—which ended in sharp headache and disordered stomach (but was not sick) and was very uncomfortable in bed till ten." But by late summer, Charles was hard at work once again on his book on coral reefs, finishing it by the end of the year.

All the while, Charles continued what he referred to as his species work. His frequent illnesses frightened him; what if he were to die before he felt his research and theories were complete enough to reveal to the world? While he and Emma visited their families in May and June of 1842, Charles wrote a draft in pencil of his five years' work on the species theory. At least something was now on paper, in case he didn't live to finish his work.

Ill health would haunt Charles for the rest of his life, frustrating him by depriving him of valuable work time and making him miserable. Modern theorists wonder, What was wrong with Darwin? Was it a disease he caught from the bite of a South American insect? A version of the family curse of intestinal distress? Could it be psychosomatic, brought about by psychological conflict over the early loss of his mother rather than by physical causes?

These questions have occupied many historians of science, and entire books have been written to bolster one or another of these ideas. Chances are, however, that Charles's illnesses were caused by a combination of factors, perhaps including a family disposition towards digestive problems combined with a psychosomatic tendency. Whatever the causes, Charles's suffering was real.

 CHAPTER NINE

A Home for a Family

CHARLES AND EMMA DECIDED to leave the stressful, dirty city of London and find a home in the country. They thought that a more peaceful environment would aid Charles's health, and that country life would be much healthier for the children. A property near a village on a train route into the city would be ideal, they thought. Charles could get into London easily when necessary, and they could raise their family in the clean, quiet, and roomy countryside.

Emma was pregnant again, with the baby due in late September 1842. The Darwins wanted to move before then, so their search intensified. In late July, they visited a property near the village of Down, sixteen miles south of London. The village wasn't on a rail line, but they saw a large house with attractive grounds, and a low price made up for the location. Traveling by carriage and then train, Charles could be in London within two hours.

Charles described the location in a letter to his sister Catherine, mentioning both pluses and minuses:

> Inhabitants [of village] very respectable.... The charm of the place to me is that almost every field is intersected (as alas is our's) by one or more footpaths—I never saw so many walks in any other country.... It is really surprising to think London is only 16 miles off.... House ugly, looks neither old nor new—Capital [meaning excellent] study 18 x 18.... plenty of bedrooms ... House in good repair.

Down House from the back, showing part of the large lawn where the children could run and play

At first, Charles hoped to rent, but that wasn't possible. His father loaned him the money, and Down House became his. Emma, almost ready to give birth, moved in September 14, and Charles followed a few days later. The baby, named Mary, was born on September 23 but lived only three weeks.

Charles reacted to the loss by throwing himself into remodeling Down House. He had rooms added to the back of the house and expanded the drawing room, and he made plans for the grounds. A kitchen garden and small orchard would help provide the family with fresh, healthy food. The ugly house quickly became the home where he and Emma would live out their lives. Not long after moving, Darwin wrote in a letter to Captain FitzRoy: "My life goes on like clockwork and I am fixed on the spot where I shall end it."

At Down, Charles continued his voluminous reading, finishing an entomology text, William Paley's *Natural Theology,* and David Hume's *History of England to Elizabeth* in six weeks from May to June of 1843. Emma was once again pregnant, and Henrietta was born on September 25. In October, the last volume of the *Beagle* zoology appeared, marking the end of a major effort for Charles. In January 1844, he finished *Geological Observations on the Volcanic Islands Visited during the Voyage of H.M.S. "Beagle."* He could now devote himself more fully to his species work.

Charles decided to tell a colleague about his species theories. He chose Joseph Dalton Hooker, a young botanist who had just come back to England from a voyage to Antarctica. Shortly after his return, Henslow had sent most of Charles's plant specimens from the *Beagle* voyage to Hooker because he couldn't find the time to examine and classify them.

Charles could not have found a better friend and colleague than Joseph Dalton Hooker. Hooker had wangled a post on James Ross's Antarctic expedition as the surgeon, which allowed him to collect plants from around the world during the four-year voyage. Botany ran in the family; Joseph's father, William, was the first director of Kew Gardens, which were to become the most famous and respected botanical gardens in the world.

After returning from the Antarctic, Joseph Hooker got a job at Kew, working with his father. He remained there for the rest of his scientific career, taking over as director in 1865. Throughout his tenure at Kew, Hooker insisted on keeping Kew primarily a research and educational institution, resisting the pressure from politicians who would have preferred a park for the pleasure of the people.

Joseph Dalton Hooker, Darwin's close friend and colleague in 1854

The Palm House at Kew Gardens, built in 1841

Today, Kew is vital for the preservation of the world's plant biodiversity, but it also serves as a popular recreational destination for the British people and tourists alike.

On January 11, 1844, Charles wrote to Joseph Hooker, beginning his letter with a few requests of things for Hooker to look for in the *Beagle* specimens and a few questions. Then he wrote:

Besides a general interest about the Southern lands, I have been now ever since my return engaged in a very presumptuous work & which I know no one individual who w^d not say a very foolish one.—I was so struck with distribution of Galapagos organisms &c &c & with the character of the American fossil mammifers [mammals], &c &c that I determined to collect blindly every sort of fact, which c^d bear any way on what are species.—I have read heaps of agricultural & horticultural books, & have never ceased collecting facts—At last gleams of light have come, & I am almost convinced (quite contrary to opinion I started with) that species are not (it is like confessing a murder) immutable. Heaven forfend me from Lamarck nonsense of a "tendency to progression" "adaptations from the slow willing of animals" &c,—but the conclusions I am led to are not widely different from his—

though the means of change are wholly so—I think I have found out (here's presumption!) the simple way by which species become exquisitely adapted to various ends.—You will now groan, & think to yourself "on what a man have I been wasting my time in writing to."—I sh^d, five years ago, have thought so. . . .

It was done. Charles had dared to tell a colleague that he was an evolutionist, and he waited nervously for Hooker's response. He must have felt tremendous relief when the reply came in a letter dated January 29. Rather than being shocked by Charles's revelation, Hooker seems to have seen it as merely mildly interesting. Most of the long letter is devoted to discussing plants. Only near the end does he respond to Charles's confession. He mentions a couple of botanical observations that seem difficult to explain if all species were created at once, then goes on to say:

> There may in my opinion have been a series of productions [creations of new species] on different spots, & also a gradual change of species. I shall be delighted to hear how you think this change may have taken place, as no presently conceived opinions satisfy me on the subject.

The matter rested there for a few months. Meanwhile, Charles had begun to elaborate on the earlier draft of his ideas. Over the next five months, he expanded the work to 230 pages, written more formally, not like personal notes. Still, he didn't feel the work was ready for publication, or even for the eyes of another scientist.

In the back of his mind, Charles always felt anxious that he might die. His ill health seemed similar to his mother's fatal illness. He addressed a letter to Emma in July, giving her instructions about what to do if he should die (no one knows if he gave her the letter):

> My dear Emma,
>   I have just finished my sketch of my species theory. If, as I believe that my theory is true & if it be accepted even by one competent judge, it will be a considerable step in science.
>   I therefore write this, in case of my sudden death, as my most solemn & last request, which I am sure you will consider the same as if legally entered

my will, that you will devote £400 to its publication & further will yourself, or through Hensleigh [her brother] take trouble in promoting it. . . .

Charles went on to tell his wife in detail how to find a "competent person" to improve and enlarge the manuscript by going through Charles's carefully annotated collection of natural-history books and notes. He suggests some possibilities, including Henslow, Joseph Hooker, Lyell, and Robert Owen. If no such person could be found, she was to have it published as is, "stating that it was done several years ago & from memory, without consulting any works & with no intention of publication in its present form." Charles feared he would be ridiculed by his colleagues even if he might no longer be alive to hear it.

After completing his species manuscript, Charles plunged into the last of three volumes on the geology of the *Beagle* voyage, finishing the first draft in April 1844. All the while, his correspondence with Hooker continued, with no mention by either one of changes in species. Charles and Emma visited Hooker in July 1844; what they talked about is not known.

In October, Charles revealed his views to yet another colleague, Leonard Jenyns, a naturalist friend from his Cambridge days who had catalogued the fish from the *Beagle* expedition. In his letter, Charles wrote:

> I have continued steadily reading & collecting facts on variation of domestic animals & plants & on the question of what are species; I have a grand body of facts & I think I can draw some sound conclusions. The general conclusions at which I have slowly been driven from a directly opposite conviction is that species are mutable & that allied species are co-descendants of common stocks. I know how much I open myself, to reproach, for such a conclusion, but have at least honestly & deliberately come to it.
>
> I shall not publish on this subject for several years—

That same month, Hooker wrote a long letter to Charles. At the very end, he expresses his own growing interest in the possibility of transmutation.

Transmutation seemed to be in the air. That same fall, an anonymous book called *Vestiges of the Natural History of Creation* was published, unleashing fevered discussion of creation versus transmutation. The book contained many interesting facts, as well as many errors. But it was written in a lively style and became so popular that three reprints came out in the first year, followed by twenty more editions in England, American publication, as well as translation into German.

Vestiges upset Charles. Here was a book about transmutation that inspired much discussion among both scientists and nonscientists alike. The book did not propose Darwin's mechanism of natural selection, but it did survey much of the same evidence from the same sources—classification, embryology, the fossil record, geology—as Charles had gathered to buttress his ideas, and *Vestiges* used them in support of the same conclusion, that species are not immutable.

Hooker wrote Charles in December 1844:

I have been delighted with *Vestiges,* from the multiplicity of facts he brings together, though I do [not] agree with his conclusions at all, he must be a funny fellow: somehow the book looks more like a 9 days wonder than a lasting work. . . . Do not think I am arguing this for the development of species!

Charles responded grouchily to Hooker: "I have also, read the *Vestiges,* but have been somewhat less amused at it, than you appear to have been: the writing & arrangement are certainly admirable, but his geology strikes me as bad, & his zoology far worse."

Meanwhile, the popular success of this book may have inspired Charles to revise his own *Journal of Researches,* his story of the voyage of the *Beagle.* By early 1845, he had in hand all the results from the experts who had examined his specimens, including the botanical results from Hooker. These especially pleased Charles, for Hooker's findings bolstered Charles's own ideas. About half his plants were unique to the Galapagos, and most occurred only on one island, evidence that after seeds had arrived by chance, the plants had changed over time to adapt to their new environments, creating new species.

Charles wrote to Hooker: "I cannot tell you how delighted & astonished I am at the results of your examination; how wonderfully they support my assertion of the differences in the animals of the different islands, about which I have always been fearful."

After finding a publisher for the revision, Charles worked hard on the project. He added more material about the Galapagos plants and animals, expanded the section on the Fuegians, and scattered hints about his new beliefs throughout the book.

Just as Charles had begun tentatively to reveal himself as an evolutionist, the *Edinburgh Review* published a blistering denunciation of *Vestiges* in July 1845. Everyone knew Darwin's former geology teacher, Adam Sedgwick, had written the review. Sedgwick railed at *Vestiges* from every angle, attacking the author as unscientific and accusing him of "rank materialism." Much of Sedgwick's wrath came from fear.

> If the book be true, the labours of sober induction are in vain; religion is a lie; human law a mass of folly and a base injustice; morality is moonshine; our labours for the black people of Africa were works of madmen; and men and women are only better beasts!

Sedgwick's attack brought out Charles's own anxiety. Such diatribes are exactly what he feared his own work would inspire when he published it. And this vicious attack came from one of his friends, from a valued member of the inner circle of British scientists.

Hooker also seemed to be having doubts. He criticized a French philosopher who wrote about transmutation. How could someone who had not worked endless hours painstakingly examining and describing specimens and separating them into describable species dare to attack the species concept, Hooker complained.

Charles took Hooker's comments personally. After all, he himself had not spent hours toiling over the minutiae of species work. He wrote to Hooker: "How painfully (to me) true is your remark that no one has hardly a right to examine the question of species who has not minutely examined many."

Hooker apologized, but Darwin's doubts had been aroused. What did he know, after all?

In October 1846, after sending the last of his third volume on geology of the *Beagle* voyage to his publisher, Charles decided it was time to try to do some species work of his own. He took out the one bottle left from his *Beagle* collection, which contained a strange kind of barnacle, a species no one had ever described before. On a visit to Down, Hooker helped Charles set up a microscope so he could study the barnacle closely. The more he looked, the more intrigued Charles became by this strange creature. The male was very tiny, and lived inside the hard, protective covering of the female, and the larva looked nothing like a barnacle. Hooker made an excellent drawing of the barnacle for Charles, and on October 26, Charles wrote a letter to Hooker full of enthusiasm:

> I have been reading heaps of papers on *Cirripedia* [the scientific name for barnacles] & your drawing is clearer than almost any of them. The more I read the more singular does our little fellow appear, & as you say, looking at its natural size, a microscope is a most wonderful instrument.

A long list of detailed questions followed.

Barnacles are indeed strange creatures. Although their solid, overlapping plates make them look like a strange sort of mollusk, barnacles are actually crustaceans, related to shrimp and crabs rather than snails and limpets. Inside the protective plates, the barnacle lies on its back. To feed, it extends its appendages, which are equivalent to the legs of a crab, through a gap in the plates and rakes the water for food. The appendages have fine bristles that filter out particles and small animals and carry them to its mouth.

Barnacles have strange reproductive patterns. Most are hermaphroditic, meaning that each animal has both male and female reproductive organs. The fact that the barnacle Charles began with had, instead, a dwarf male that lived inside the female's plates, is part of what intrigued Charles about the creature.

Many barnacles have become parasites, living inside the bodies of other animals, such as crabs. These species completely lack plates, and their saclike or branched bodies make them totally unrecognizable. Only their young, called larvae, give away their biological relationship to familiar barnacles.

Charles had become entranced by barnacles and all their oddities. Barnacles clearly needed to be studied systematically, which would give Charles the experience in species work he now felt was needed. And perhaps he felt relieved to be pursuing this research instead of forging ahead with his unorthodox evolutionary ideas. Without realizing that it would take him eight difficult years, he launched into a complete study of these peculiar animals.

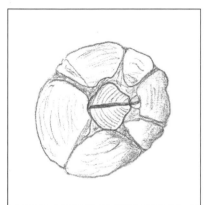

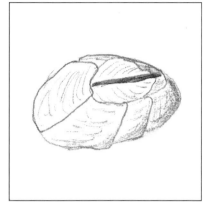

Barnacles are very common animals often found clinging to ships and to rocks on the ocean shore. The top view on the left shows how the barnacle closes up tight to protect itself from preditors or from drying out. The middle drawing shows how the center plates open up so the animal can feed. On the right is a differend kind of barnacle.

 CHAPTER TEN

At Home with the Darwins

B Y 1847, CHARLES HAD SETTLED into the life of a country gentleman. After the dirt and noise of London, he relished the serenity of Down. The peace and quiet of country living proved essential to the success of Darwin's career. He needed to be insulated from the confusion and demands of city life.

Most families like the Darwins had a houseful of servants, so Emma had plenty of help at Down. Charles's butler, Joseph Parslow, oversaw the male staff, while the housekeeper managed the female servants. Servants carried out all the manual labor—tending to the garden and the animals, hauling coal for the stoves and water for washing, laying out clothes for their masters, laundering, keeping the house spic and span, cooking, cleaning up after meals, and so forth. The children had their nanny and their governess to take care of them and educate them. The staff of servants left Charles free of domestic responsibilities so he could do his work and allowed Emma to devote her attention to Charles.

The house may have been plain, but remodeling to suit the family had made it very livable. Charles had arranged the "capital study" to suit him, putting in special shelves that served as a filing cabinet for his extensive notes. He filled the bookcase with volumes covering the breadth of human learning—*The History of the Mongols, Das Kapital, The Supernatural in Nature, Scotch Deer-Hounds and Their Masters,* and *The Morality of Nations* all found their way to his shelves.

A vital part of Charles's creative life was the sandwalk. He bought a strip of land along the border of the fifteen-acre meadow behind his house where oaks and shrubs grew. He added other trees such as birch and dogwood, and Emma contributed flowers. A sandy path was made forming a loop trail around the woods. On the far side, the path bordered a neighbor's meadow across which Charles could see a peaceful valley. After the sharp turn at the far end of the loop lay a view of the fields of Down House itself and the countryside beyond.

The beloved sandwalk, where Charles strolled to relax and to think

As Charles strolled the sandwalk with his dog, he could choose between broad vistas on one side and dark woods along the other. For most of his years at Down, Charles kicked a stone from a small pile into the path every time he returned to the beginning of the loop to keep track of how many times he had gone around. The sand path provided a place where Charles could rest his active mind or stimulate it with the sights, sounds, and smells that surrounded him. Many of his ideas came to him as he walked there.

The family routine at Down focused on Charles's needs. He settled into a precise daily schedule. Only when he was away from home or when he became ill did Charles deviate from his routine. After dressing in the morning, he took a stroll around the sandwalk, then ate breakfast at 7:45. From 8:00 to 9:30 A.M., he worked in his study. These early hours, when his mind was fresh, were his most productive time. At 9:30, Charles would rest on the couch in the drawing room while Emma read to him from family letters or popular novels. They both loved Jane Austen's books.

Charles went back to work from 10:30 to noon, when he took another walk and, later in life, checked on the plants in his greenhouse, which was built in 1863. Lunch, the main meal of the day, was served precisely at 1:00, after which Charles would read the newspaper, the only nonscientific reading he did by himself. Then he answered letters until 3:00.

In those days, mail was delivered several times a day, and country gentlemen like Charles devoted a great deal of time to reading and writing letters. During Darwin's lifetime, letters comprised the common means of communication, since telephones had not been invented yet. Up until 1840, sending letters was expensive, with postage based on how far in England the letter traveled. A letter consisted of a single sheet of paper, with writing on one side, that was folded and sealed using a gummed wafer or a waxed seal. Any enclosure doubled the postage. Because of the cost of letters, abbreviated sentences and words were normal, such as the & for *and* seen in so many letters quoted here.

In 1840, the penny-post came into being. A letter could then be sent anywhere in England for a penny for each half ounce. Envelopes also came into more common use at that time.

Charles Darwin carried on an extraordinary correspondence with family and with colleagues. Of the fourteen thousand letters to and from Darwin still known to exist, about nine thousand of them rest in the archives of the

Cambridge University Library. One by one, the letters are being transcribed word for word, misspellings and all, by a crew of dedicated people. The first volume of the *Correspondence of Charles Darwin,* covering 1821 to 1836, was published in 1985. Volume 10, which covers 1862, came out in 1997. Thanks to the publication of these letters, we are able to get an unprecedented look at the life of one of the nineteenth century's most important people and at the lives of those with whom he corresponded.

After finishing his correspondence, Charles retired to the bedroom to smoke while Emma once again read to him. When 4:00 arrived, it was time for another tour around the sandwalk, followed sometimes by an hour of work, a smoke, and another session of listening to Emma read or play the piano.

Following a simple meal at 7:30, the Darwins retired again to the drawing room to play backgammon and enjoy more of Emma's piano playing. The day ended by 10:30 P.M.

The drawing room at Down House, center of Darwin family life

Life at Down allowed Charles to focus on his work. Routine anchored him and he realized he thought best in the company of nature along his sand-walk. Distractions were minimal, and his needs were consistently met by others. He didn't have to worry about making a living, so he could devote his time to his scientific pursuits. He also had a pool table installed in the room next to his study. When he needed a break, all he had to do was summon his butler, Parslow, for a game of billiards, which would "drive the horrid species out of my head" while he wrestled with his evolutionary ideas.

When Charles began his barnacle work at age thirty-seven, Emma was once again pregnant. By then, he and Emma had four living children: William, almost seven; Annie, five; Henrietta, three; and George, fifteen months. The new baby, Elizabeth (called Bessy), was born on July 8, 1847. In those days, large families were the norm. Four more children, all sons, would follow: Francis (born August 16, 1848), Leonard (born January 15, 1850), Horace (born May 13, 1851), and Charles Waring (born December 6, 1856).

Fathers in Victorian England generally took little interest in their children, but Charles enjoyed fatherhood immensely and doted on his offspring. His children remembered his patience and his kindness. His son Francis quotes his sister Henrietta in *The Life of Charles Darwin:*

> My first remembrances of my father are of the delights of his playing with us. . . . To all of us he was the most delightful play-fellow, and the most perfect sympathiser. Indeed it is impossible adequately to describe how delightful a relation his was to his family, whether as children or in their later life.

Charles found it difficult to say no to his children. The children were even allowed to play in his study, and they relished pushing one another around the room on the three-wheeled stool Charles used when examining specimens with his microscope.

Henrietta continued:

> He cared for all our pursuits and interests, and lived our lives with us in a way that very few fathers do. But I am certain that none of us felt that this intimacy interfered the least with our respect and obedience. Whatever he said was absolute truth and law to us.

In the same book, Francis wrote: "The Sandwalk was our play-ground as children, and here we continually saw my father as he walked round. He liked to see what we were doing, and was ever ready to sympathize in any fun that was going on."

The children always knew what their father was up to and considered their life to be normal. While visiting a friend's house, one of Charles's sons asked, "When does your father do his barnacles?" The children also helped in Charles's experiments. When their father was studying worms, the children helped him test what sounds the worms could hear by playing their musical instruments and making noises. Horace helped make observations on how worms displace soil. Francis became fascinated by the movements of plants his father studied and eventually became a plant physiologist himself.

Charles also respected his offspring as individuals. In Henrietta's words, again quoted in her brother's book: "[H]e always made us feel that we were each of us creatures whose opinions and thoughts were valuable to him, so that whatever there was best in us came out in the sunshine of his presence."

Even though he was a loving and attentive father, Charles sometimes observed his children's behavior with scientific detachment. When his first child, William, was born in 1839, Charles began keeping a notebook on his development, mixing fatherly pride in with careful observation:

During the first week, [William] yawned streatched himself just like old person—chiefly upper extremities—hiccupped—sneezes sucked, Surface of warm hand placed to face, seemed immediately to give wish of sucking, either instinctive or associated knowledge of warm smooth surface of bosom.— Cried & squalled, but no tears . . .

A letter to Fox in June 1840 showed Charles's delight in fatherhood:

[William] is a prodigy of beauty & intellect. He is so charming that I cannot pretend to any modesty.—I defy anybody to flatter us on our baby,—for I defy anyone to say anything, in its praise, of which we are not fully conscious.—

He is a charming little fellow, & I had not the smallest concepcion there was so much in a five month baby. . . .

Much later in life, when Charles wrote one of his most important books, *The Expression of the Emotions in Man and Animals,* he used his observations of William's behavior in the text.

The years passed and Charles worked hard, but the Darwins also took vacations to visit family members. Now and then, Charles visited London to spend time with Erasmus and with his colleagues or to conduct other business, but he always returned as quickly as possible. Work on the barnacles took up most of his professional time.

Illness, however, continued to plague Charles. He calculated that, in total, he lost two of the eight years of barnacle research to sickness. At the end of 1848, he wrote in his diary, "From July to end of year, unusually unwell, with swimming of head, depression, trembling—many bad attacks of sickness."

That year had been especially difficult for Charles. By the summer of 1848, his father, who had been suffering heart trouble for several years, had begun to talk of his own impending death. When Charles visited The Mount in October, it became clear his father wouldn't live much longer. On November 13, Robert Waring Darwin died. Charles, although feeling very sick himself, traveled to London, where his brother Erasmus joined him for the sad journey to Shrewsbury. Charles and his eldest sister, Marianne, were both too ill to attend the funeral.

After his father's death, Charles couldn't shake his feelings of depression. In February he wrote to Fox, "[A]ll the autumn and winter I have been much dispirited and inclined to do nothing but what I was forced to do."

Charles continued to be troubled by his own health problems. The primitive state of medicine during the nineteenth century meant that little could be done for most serious illnesses. The modern arsenal of immunization, antibiotics, chemotherapy, and so forth, did not exist then. As a result, many supposed "cures" came into being. The list of treatments used on Darwin's mysterious illness shows how little was understood about his disease. It included amyl nitrite, arsenic, batteries, bismuth, diets, "electric chains," Indian ale, morphine, quinine, and tartar emetic ointment, which induces vomiting!

Natural hot springs were believed to help treat a variety of diseases, and people traveled from all over England to towns such as Bath, Ilkley, and Malvern in hopes of improvement.

Charles's problems became bad enough that in March 1849 he and the entire household traveled to Malvern. There, a doctor named Gully offered a "water cure," which Charles hoped would stem his "incessant vomiting." The cure involved wearing a cold, wet compress almost the entire day, being scrubbed with cold water, and putting his feet into cold water, as well as a strict diet. The rules forbade sugar, butter, spices, tea, bacon, or "anything good," according to Charles. The family spent more than three months at Malvern before returning to Down, with Charles feeling much better.

Charles installed equipment at home so he could continue with the water cure. He also kept detailed notes of the state of his health. This diary, started in January 1849, lasted for six years. In July, Charles finally got back to his barnacle work.

The next year, disaster struck. Charles's nine-year-old daughter Annie became ill. She and her governess were sent to the coastal town of Ramsgate, a popular place for the ill to recuperate, but she didn't get better. In March 1851, she began vomiting, and Charles took her to Malvern and left her there with her sister Henrietta, her governess, and the family nanny, Brodie. Charles hoped Dr. Gully could make his daughter well.

Nothing helped, and Annie's condition grew worse. In April, Charles returned to Malvern to find Annie gaunt and feverish. On April 23, she died. Heartbroken, Charles returned to Down, where Emma gave birth to Horace three weeks later.

Annie Darwin at age 8, beloved daughter who died in 1851

Annie's death devastated both Charles and Emma. After her death, Charles wrote a memoir of Annie to keep her memory alive. The last paragraph reads: "We have lost the joy of the household, and the solace of our old age. Oh that she could now know how deeply, how tenderly we do still & shall ever love her dear joyous face."

Brodie, the nanny, became so immersed in grief that she had to leave the family and retire, and Charles refused ever to visit Annie's simple grave in Malvern. He never spoke of her in later years. The pain was too great.

After Annie died, Charles worried greatly about his other children. He was convinced that she had inherited his own ill health and that the others could also become sick. Would his surviving children live into adulthood?

Women and children were especially vulnerable to early death. As late as 1870, 1 birth in 204 in England resulted in the death of the mother. Considering the number of children each woman bore, her chances of dying were quite high. Children were especially susceptible to certain diseases, such as diphtheria and scarlet fever.

Other illnesses took everyone. Untreated typhoid fever killed one in four victims. Cholera, which originated in Asia, came to Europe in the 1830s. From then on, periodic deadly epidemics struck that could spread rapidly. But the greatest killer of all, until antibiotics came into use in the middle of the twentieth century, was tuberculosis. Sixty thousand people died from this disease in Britain between 1838 and 1843.

Charles's concern about his children's future also extended to their schooling. A traditional British education had been a disaster for him. But could his boys obtain good jobs and succeed in society if they did not follow a traditional path? "I cannot endure to think of sending my boys to waste 7 of 8 years in making miserable Latin verses," he wrote to Fox in September 1850, but he continued, "I feel that it is an awful experiment to depart from the usual course, however bad that course may be." Charles even thought about emigrating to Australia or America, where the children would not be burdened by the outdated British system of education.

William was now almost eleven, and it was time for him to graduate from home tutoring to a regular school. Charles and Emma looked into an alternative school but finally took the conservative course and sent William to Rugby, a highly respected public school.

Charles continued his barnacle work, bit by bit examining specimens and figuring out relationships. In March 1852, he described his routine in a letter to Fox:

> I dread going anywhere on account of my stomach so easily failing under any excitement. I rarely even now go to London, not that I am at all worse, perhaps rather better and lead a very comfortable life with my 3 hours of daily work, but it is the life of a hermit. My nights are *always* bad, and that stops my becoming vigorous.

Charles and Emma did make family visits, and now and then, Charles braved the trip to London. However, travel did not agree with Charles. In October, he wrote in a letter to Fox, "The other day I went to London and back, and the fatigue, though so trifling, brought on a very bad form of vomiting."

As 1852 drew to a close, Charles could finally see the end to his seemingly endless barnacle study. One volume on fossil barnacles had been published the previous year, and he had completed most of the remaining research. By this time, Charles could hardly stand to think of barnacles. "I hate a Barnacle as no man ever did before, not even a sailor in a slow moving ship," he complained in a letter to Fox.

Even though it took eight long years of his life, the barnacle work contributed greatly to Charles's reputation, helped him improve his skills as a scientist, and aided him in refining his evolutionary ideas. At the end of 1853, the Royal Society awarded him its prestigious Royal Medal for his work on coral reefs and barnacles. Charles was pleased, but the congratulations he received from friends such as Hooker meant even more to him. His health also improved. In April 1854, he was elected to the Philosophical Club, founded by members of the Royal Society who wanted to stimulate discussion of interesting ideas.

That year, Charles traveled often to London to attend meetings of the Philosophical Club and the Royal Society. He continued his voracious reading and kept up his scientific correspondence, especially with Hooker. In September, he packed up his barnacles and sent away the final proofs for the last barnacle volume. The time had come to return to his difficult theoretical work.

CHAPTER ELEVEN

Putting It All Together

THE FINAL ENTRY IN CHARLES'S DIARY for September 9, 1854, reads, "Began sorting notes for species theory." Charles had finally returned to his long-ignored theoretical work on species. The barnacles had taken eight years of his life but had given him firsthand experience with the problems of biological classification, such as distinguishing between species and varieties. Charles now considered himself to be a professional naturalist who could cite his personal research in support of his theories. He now had the credentials to complete and present his ideas.

In his 1844 essay, Darwin had written that variation occurred only when species were subjected to changes in their environment. For example, he believed that when land rose or subsided, the change in elevation would alter the climate, stimulating organisms to vary; then natural selection would favor the individuals best adapted to the new conditions. Bringing plants and animals into domestication also changed their environment, stimulating variation, Darwin thought. These variations could then be selected by people to create new breeds and varieties.

Charles's work with barnacles forced him to rethink his idea. He had thought that individuals within a species varied only when the environment changed. But when he examined barnacles, he consistently found a great deal of natural variation in different individuals of the same species. Variation was normal, he reasoned, not something that came about only when the environment changed.

It wasn't long before Charles realized his theory was incomplete in another way. As paleontologists uncovered more and more fossils, Darwin saw that over time, groups of animals kept diverging from one another, becoming more and more specialized. Until he could explain how major groups such as horses and camels, or wolves and bears, had diverged from one another, he didn't want to publish his ideas. He believed that his theory needed to explain evolution both on the small and the large scale, in stable environments as well as new ones.

In November 1854, Darwin realized why species kept changing. "I can remember the very spot in the road, whilst in my carriage, when to my joy the solution occurred to me," he wrote in his autobiography. The result was his "principle of divergence." Charles realized that the environment offered many ways for plants and animals to "make a living." And since variations in the organisms were always present, any variation that enabled an individual to utilize a resource more effectively would be preserved. For example, a bird with a larger than average beak could feed better on big seeds and would choose them, while one with a smaller beak could utilize smaller seeds more easily. Each kind of bird could specialize, increasing its chance to survive and reproduce. Large- and small-beaked birds could share the same environment, since they wouldn't compete for food. Over time, both larger and smaller beaks would be preserved, widening the differences between the birds.

Eventually, Darwin decided, differences would accumulate until the birds became separate species. The same principle would apply on a larger scale. Over very long periods of time, more and more changes would lead to animals as different as horses and camels, or wolves and bears.

In order to challenge the idea that God created all the species and placed them where they could thrive, Charles had to show that individuals from the mainland could get to isolated environments such as islands to colonize them. By the mid-1850s, Charles Lyell's work had become so influential that his theory about "land bridges" had become the accepted explanation of how plants and animals got from one place to another. According to this theory, there once had been a peninsula everywhere there were islands now.

Charles began to challenge this idea and examine how organisms could cross the water to colonize volcanic islands. He realized that the Galapagos Islands, for example, were too far from the South American mainland to have once been connected by a land bridge. He believed animals and the seeds of plants had gotten there some other way.

Charles's friend and colleague Joseph Hooker agreed with most naturalists that connections to land had brought plants to islands. Charles was determined to overcome his friend's skepticism. As Charles wrote to Hooker in June 1855:

> I cannot make exactly out why you w^d prefer continental transmission, as I think you do. . . . For my own pet theoretical notions, it is quite indifferent whether they are transmitted by sea or land, as long as some, tolerably probable way is shown. But it shocks my philosophy to create land, without some other & independent evidence.

Charles had to find that "tolerably probable" means of getting seeds to islands. Perhaps seeds could float there. But then, they would have to survive being soaked in salt water, and Charles would have to show that they could. Even though he disagreed with Darwin, Hooker helped him. He told Charles which plants grew on which islands, and he provided Charles with many seeds.

In a letter of April 19, 1855, Charles described his setup to Hooker: "I shall keep the great receptacle with salt-water with 40 or 50 little bottles, partly open, immersed in it in the cellar, for uniform temperature.—I must plant out of doors, as I have no green House."

On April 24, after some success with a preliminary group of seeds, Charles wrote gleefully: "You are a good man to confess that you expected the crop w^d be killed in a week, for this gives me a nice little triumph. The children at first were tremendously eager & asked me often 'whether I sh^d beat D^r. Hooker?'!!"

Charles's glee didn't last long. Most of the seeds sank, and sunken seeds wouldn't make it to islands. If seeds sank, maybe seed pods or entire plants, perhaps uprooted in a storm, would float. After many experiments, Charles found that dried branches of hazelnuts carrying seeds could float for ninety days, and the seeds could germinate afterwards. When Charles checked the speed of the Atlantic currents, he found that in twenty-eight days, the seeds could travel over nine hundred miles, far enough to colonize islands even farther from shore than the Galapagos.

But Charles still wasn't content. He wanted to find as many ways as possible for seeds to reach new land, and he also needed to prove that land animals could get there. Birds, he reasoned, could bring seeds and small creatures that clung to their feet to islands. He experimented with a pair of duck feet, submerging them in an aquarium containing freshwater snails, then removing the feet from the water. He waved the feet in the air as if the bird were flying, then kept them out of the water for hours to see how long the snails could survive. Charles enlisted his children to count the number of snails that clung to the feet. From these experiments, Charles concluded that a bird could fly as far as seven hundred miles carrying snails to new waters when the bird landed. The children also helped Charles find other ways for transporting new life to islands. In a letter to Hooker in 1856, Charles recounts:

> I must tell you another of my *profound* experiments! Franky [son Francis] said to me, "why sh^d not a bird be killed (by hawk, lightning, apoplexy, hail & c) with seeds in crop [a throat pouch where birds store food], & would swim." No sooner said, than done: a pigeon has floated for 30 days in salt water with seeds in crop & they have grown splendidly.

Charles also studied domesticated animals in detail to help refine his theories. He believed that by investigating the artificial selection breeders had made to preserve desired traits, he could learn something about natural selection in nature. He wrote letters to William Tegetmeir, a man who knew nearly everyone who bred poultry, especially fancy pigeons. Charles wanted to focus on pigeons, as an amazing number of striking varieties had been developed through conscious selection in captivity.

The familiar city pigeon is the descendant of escaped domesticated pigeons. Long ago, a wild species called the rock dove came to live in cities, which mimicked its natural environment of rocky cliffs that bordered open fields. Over time, people tamed the pigeon and used its eggs and young for food. People as far back as the ancient Greeks have taken advantage of the homing ability of pigeons, using them to carry messages from place to place.

During the thousands of years pigeons have lived with humans, more than two hundred basic breeds have been developed. Within each breed are still more variations. Charles chose to study pigeons in detail because of these variations, both within and among the breeds.

Charles began keeping his own pigeons and fancy barnyard birds. He had as many as sixteen different pigeon breeds and up to nine kinds of poultry at one time. If people could select desired traits in their domesticated animals and then breed them so that these traits were passed on to the next generation, nature could surely do the same thing. In nature, what Charles called "the conditions of life" would take the place of the human breeder, weeding out traits that were not well adapted and preserving those that were.

Pigeons also helped Charles demonstrate another important point. Some people believed that different wild species had given rise to the fancy breeds. Charles set out to show that only one species, the wild rock dove, was ancestor to all the strikingly different kinds of domesticated pigeons. He wrote of his studies in *The Origin of Species*, explaining that when he measured various parts of nestlings of different breeds, they differed far less than they did in the adults. He considered this evidence that the breeds had all been developed from the same species.

While he gathered evidence for his ideas, Charles kept in close contact with his colleagues and friends, especially Henslow, Hooker, and Lyell. Charles knew he would need backing from other respected scientists once he published his findings. He also made two new scientific friends who would prove to be very important in the future. While on a visit to London in April 1853, Charles met a young comparative anatomist named Thomas Huxley. Starting in 1846, Huxley had traveled on a Royal Navy surveying trip as the surgeon and used the opportunity to collect specimens of marine invertebrate animals. His close study of these neglected creatures resulted in scientific papers that made his reputation as a naturalist before the ship reached home in 1850.

Born to a poor family, Huxley had to hustle to make a living, and finally received an appointment at the School of Mines and Museum of Practical Geology in London. He also became the paleontologist to the Geological Survey. Huxley and Darwin corresponded regularly and, after publication of *The Origin of Species*, Huxley became Darwin's most vocal defender.

In 1855, Charles began corresponding with a prominent American botanist, Asa Gray. Gray was fascinated by the species question, and in 1856, Charles told Gray of his research on this problem and mentions his own "heterodox conclusions." Gray's answer expressed interest in Charles's ideas, and in September 1857, Darwin wrote back with a brief outline of his theory. Charles couldn't know it at the time, but that letter would play a key role in his scientific career.

The most important new figure in Charles's life, however, was a young naturalist named Alfred Russel Wallace, born in 1823 to a poor family. He had to quit school at the age of thirteen and worked in a carpenter's shop in London for a year, then worked for five years with a brother who was a surveyor. Young Alfred became an enthusiastic naturalist, devouring every book he could find on foreign expeditions. Like Darwin, Wallace read Humboldt's *Travels in South America.* That book, combined with Charles's own *Journal of Researches* (the 1845 edition) made Wallace determined to go on his own tropical adventures. When Wallace read *Vestiges of Creation,* the anonymously written book that had so annoyed Charles, he became an evolutionist.

In 1847, Wallace headed for the Amazon with fellow naturalist Henry Walter Bates, who would later become famous. The two planned to collect animals, largely insects, and sell specimens to support themselves. Wallace

"Darwin's bulldog," Thomas Henry Huxley, in 1891, and Alfred Russel Wallace, who also came up with the concept of natural selection, photographed in 1866

also wanted to solve the species problem. After four years of hardship and adventure, he headed home. The ship caught fire, and Wallace escaped with his life but lost his precious collection. The collection was insured, but the scientific loss was incalculable.

While in England, Wallace presented papers to scientific societies and began to establish a reputation. But only fifteen months after his return, in early 1854, he traveled to the islands of present-day Indonesia. He would be gone for eight years. While in the Amazon and Indonesia, Wallace devoted a lot of time to thinking about mechanisms for evolution.

CHAPTER TWELVE

Transmutation in the Air

ALFRED RUSSEL WALLACE published a paper, "On the Law Which Has Regulated the Introduction of New Species," in 1855. He had been thinking hard about the species problem, and this paper discussed some of his preliminary ideas. When Lyell read it, he was sufficiently impressed that he began his own species journal.

Lyell visited Charles in April 1856 and asked if Charles had read Wallace's paper. In his response, Darwin finally told his colleague about his own theory of natural selection. Realizing that Wallace was thinking much like Darwin, Lyell pleaded with Charles in a May 1 letter: "I wish you would publish some small fragment of your data pigeons if you please & so out with the theory & let it take date—& be cited—& understood."

Charles, however, couldn't bring himself to publish an incomplete manuscript. "With respect to your suggestion of a sketch of my view," he wrote to Lyell,

> I hardly know what to think, but will reflect on it; but it goes against my prejudices. To give a fair sketch would be absolutely impossible, for every proposition requires such an array of facts. . . . I rather hate the idea of writing for priority, yet I certainly sh^d be vexed if any one were to publish my doctrines before me.

Darwin's mentor and friend, Charles Lyell, in 1855

Spurred on by Lyell, Charles did begin work on a "Big Book" for publication called "Natural Selection." Charles worked hard, finishing two chapters by mid-October and another by mid-December. Four more chapters were written by early April 1857, and Charles continued to work steadily on the project.

In October 1856, Alfred Wallace wrote to Darwin. The two men had already been in correspondence, for Charles had asked Wallace to send him specimens of wild and domestic fowl from Malaysia. Charles received Wallace's letter, which had traveled thousands of miles, in May of 1857 and responded promptly, referring both to the letter and to Wallace's earlier paper: "I can plainly see that we have thought much alike & I daresay that you will agree with me that it is very rare to find oneself agreeing pretty closely with any theoretical paper."

Although he encouraged Wallace, Charles was careful not to reveal his own ideas: "It is really *impossible* to explain my views in the compass of a letter on the causes & means of variation in a state of nature; but I have slowly adopted a distinct & tangible idea."

Wallace replied, and Darwin answered him again in December 1857. Then in June 1858, Darwin received the bombshell—a letter from Wallace enclosing an essay entitled "On the Tendency of Varieties to Depart Indefinitely from the Original Type." (Both the letter and the essay sent to Darwin have disappeared, but a version of the essay was published in 1859.) Wallace had independently reached the same idea as Darwin's concept of natural selection. In his autobiography, written in 1905, Wallace describes how it happened during an attack of fever:

> I had nothing to do but to think over any subjects then particularly interesting to me. One day something brought to my recollection Malthus's "Principles of Population," which I had read about twelve years before. I thought of his clear exposition of "the positive checks to increase"—disease, accidents, war, and famine. . . . It then occurred to me that these causes or their equivalents are continually acting in the case of animals also. . . . Vaguely thinking over the enormous and constant destruction which this implied, it occurred to me to ask the question, Why do some die and some live? And the answer was clearly, that on the whole the best fitted live. . . . Then it suddenly flashed upon me that this self-acting process would necessarily *improve the race,* because in every generation the inferior would inevitably be killed off and the superior would remain—that is, *the fittest would survive. . . .*

Charles was thunderstruck. Wallace had arrived at the same conclusions as he had twenty years earlier. He immediately forwarded the letter and the paper to Lyell, writing in his accompanying note:

> Some year or so ago, you recommended me to read a paper by Wallace in the Annals, which had interested you & as I was writing to him, I knew this would please him much, so I told him. He has to day sent me the enclosed & asked me to forward it to you. It seems to me well worth reading. Your words have come true with a vengeance that I sh^d be forestalled. You said this when I explained to you here very briefly my views of "Natural Selection" depending on the Struggle for existence.—I never saw a more striking coincidence. If Wallace had my M.S. Sketch written out in 1842 he could not have made a better short abstract! Even his terms now stand as Heads of my Chapters.

Please return me the M.S. Which he does not say he wishes me to publish; but I shall of course at once write & offer to send to any Journal. So all my originality, whatever it may amount to, will be smashed. Though my Book, if it will ever have any value, will not be deteriorated; as all the labour consists in the application of the theory.

Charles was distressed about Wallace's work. What should he do? Could he honorably publish his own ideas now? A week after sending Wallace's material to Lyell, Charles wrote once again to the great geologist:

I sh^d be *extremely* glad **now** to publish a sketch of my general views in about a dozen pages or so. . . . But as I had not intended to publish any sketch, can I do so honourably because Wallace has sent me an outline of his doctrine?— I would far rather burn my whole book than that he or any man sh^d think that I had behaved in a paltry spirit. Do you not think his having sent me this sketch ties my hands? . . .

This letter is miserably written & I write it now, that I may for time banish whole subject. And I am worn out with musing. . . .

My good dear friend forgive me. . . .

Charles asked Lyell to confer with Hooker, and the two men came up with a plan. They suggested submitting Wallace's paper along with some of Darwin's writing to the Linnaean Society as a joint paper. This would honorably solve the problem; Wallace's formulation would be presented, but the fact that Charles had come up with the same idea and had been exploring it for twenty years would also become known. The letter Charles wrote to Asa Gray in 1857 explaining natural selection would be proof.

While Charles was agonizing about this moral dilemma, his daughter Henrietta had a serious illness, and the youngest child, Charles Waring, also became ill. On June 28, in the middle of all the correspondence with Lyell and Hooker, Charles and Emma's youngest child died, at the age of only eighteen months. Faced with personal tragedy, Charles couldn't deal with the complex moral problems posed by Wallace's paper. When Hooker wrote to him, apparently urging a quick response in order to resolve the issue, Darwin wrote back:

I have just read your letter, & see you want papers at once. I am quite prostrated & can do nothing but I send Wallace & my abstract of abstract of letter to Asa Gray. . . . I daresay all is too late. I hardly care about it—. . . .

Do not waste much time. It is miserable in me to care at all about priority.

Hooker and Lyell handled everything from then on. On June 30, 1858, they forwarded material to the Linnaean Society—excerpts from Darwin's 1844 abstract, an abstract of the 1857 letter to Asa Gray, and Wallace's essay. The material was presented on July 1.

Meanwhile, potentially deadly scarlet fever was spreading through the Darwin household, and Charles was far more concerned about his family's survival than the question of scientific priority.

By July 13, the health crisis in the Darwin household had subsided, and Charles was able to communicate more normally in a letter to Hooker.

I always thought it very possible that I might be forestalled, but I fancied that I had grand enough soul not to care; but I found myself mistaken & punished; I had, however, quite resigned myself & had written half a letter to Wallace to give up all priority to him & sh^d certainly not have changed had it not been for Lyell's & yours quite extraordinary kindness. . . .

I am **much** *more* than satisfied at what took place at Linn. Soc^y. . . . Whenever naturalists can look at species changing as certain, what a magnificent field will be open,—on all the laws of variation,—on the genealogy of all living beings. . . .

Wallace was also happy about the result. Hooker wrote to him explaining how his and Charles's material would be presented to the Linnaean Society, and Charles sent it on, along with his own letter. Neither letter survives, but Wallace wrote to his mother:

I have received letters from Mr. Darwin and Dr. Hooker, two of the most eminent naturalists in England, which have highly gratified me. I sent Mr. Darwin an essay on a subject upon which he is now writing a great work. He showed it to Dr. Hooker and Sir Charles Lyell, who thought so highly of it that they had it read before the Linnaean Society. This insures me the acquaintance of these eminent men on my return home.

The scientific world took little notice of the Linnaean Society presentation. As a matter of fact, the president of the society complained at the annual meeting that the year 1858 had not seen the presentation of any striking discoveries.

Darwin and Wallace corresponded sporadically until 1862, when Wallace returned from the Malay archipelago. They met for the first time in the summer of that year. Wallace lived in London, and he and Darwin got together only about once a year, when Charles came to London to visit his brother, Erasmus. While both men claimed in 1858 that their theories were virtually identical, major differences became clear as they each refined their ideas over the years.

Through letters and scientific papers, Darwin and Wallace tried to resolve the differences in their theories about how evolution operates. They had great mutual respect, but neither could convince the other. Darwin was especially upset about their differences. In 1868, he wrote to Wallace: "I grieve to differ from you, and it actually terrifies me, and makes me constantly distrust myself. I fear we shall never quite understand each other."

Today, biologists are not surprised that the two great theorists could not agree; some of the very same arguments rage today, despite the tremendous amount of knowledge about heredity and evolution that has accumulated since their time. For example, Darwin believed that natural selection operates on individuals, with a few possible exceptions. Wallace, on the other hand, believed that natural selection often operates on groups of organisms as well as on individuals. Evolutionists today still debate the relative importance of individual versus group selection.

CHAPTER THIRTEEN

The Origin of Species

WHILE LYELL AND HOOKER worked on and presented the compromise, Charles struggled to keep his family safe. After the baby's death, Charles sent all the children, except for Henrietta, to the home of Emma's sister, Elizabeth. Charles and Emma stayed in Down to care for Henrietta and two nursemaids who had also become ill. Once Henrietta became well enough to travel, the whole family retreated to the Isle of Wight, hoping to escape the scarlet fever epidemic in Down.

Shortly after they arrived on the island, Charles's colleagues convinced him to write about natural selection for rapid publication. His big book would have to wait. Perhaps a series of papers for the *Linnaean Journal* would do. On July 20, 1858, Charles began what he called his "Abstract." On July 30, he wrote to Hooker:

> This is a very charming place & we have got a very comfortable house. But alas I cannot say that the sea has done Etty [Henrietta] or Lenny [Leonard] much good. [Leonard had been chronically ill.] Nor has my stomach recovered all our troubles. I am very glad we left home, for six children have now died of Scarlet Fever in Down. . . .
>
> I pass my time by doing daily a couple of hours of my Abstract & I find it amusing & improving work. I am now *most hea[r]tily* obliged to you & Lyell for having set me on this. . . .

Henrietta Darwin, often sickly daughter of Charles and Emma, in 1856

Charles continued to work on the abstract after returning home. He soon realized that a series of papers wouldn't do; he had to write a book. He wrote and edited furiously, mercilessly cutting what he'd already written for the "Big Book" and adding new material to complete the argument.

In April 1859, Charles arranged for publication of the work. He wanted to use the title "An Abstract of an Essay on the Origin of Species and Varieties through Natural Selection," but the publisher insisted on the short main title, "On the Origin of Species" with "by Means of Natural Selection" in smaller type below.

In a letter to Lyell before publication, Charles worried about whether the publisher, John Murray, would hesitate because of the book's content:

Would you advise me to tell Murray that my Book is not more *un*orthodox, than the subject makes inevitable. That I do not discuss origin of man.—That

I do not bring in any discussions about Genesis &c, & only give facts, & such conclusions from them, as seem to me fair.—

Or had I better say *nothing* to Murray, & assume that he cannot object to this much unorthodoxy, which in fact is not more than any Geological Treatise, which runs slap counter to Genesis. [By saying that the earth is millions of years old and that fossils can be that old, geologists ran counter to the Church of England doctrine that the earth was only thousands of years old.]

The manuscript went off to the publisher before the end of April 1859. When Charles received the proofs in June, he insisted on making many revisions to clarify what he saw as his own bad and unclear writing. He finished them by October 1, and on November 24, the book was published. The print run of 1,250 copies sold out the first day.

The Origin of Species is divided into three sections. In the first, Darwin

Charles in 1854, after finishing his long work on barnacles

introduces the theory of natural selection. He begins by discussing domesticated animals and plants. He realized that people were more familiar with barnyard animals and garden plants than with wild organisms, so he wanted to start with something they knew. If he could get his readers to understand artificial selection by breeders, he was on the way to getting them to accept natural selection in nature.

Not knowing how traits are passed from parents to offspring hampered Darwin's work. He had found variability in barnacles living in stable conditions. Even so, he couldn't give up the idea that changed conditions resulted in increased variation. Otherwise, why did domesticated plants and animals vary so greatly?

In chapter 2, "Variation under Nature," Darwin tried to convince the reader that what naturalists called "varieties" of a species could be new species in the making. Often, he noted, scientists couldn't even agree on whether a given form is a species or a variety:

> [I]n determining whether a form should be ranked as a species or a variety, the opinion of naturalists having sound judgment and wide experience seems the only guide to follow. We must, however, in many cases, decide by a majority of naturalists, for few well-marked and well-known varieties can be named which have not been ranked as species by at least some competent judges.

Chapter 3 introduced the "Struggle for Existence." Darwin pointed out that this term included many different "struggles":

> Two canine animals, in a time of dearth, may be truly said to struggle with each other which shall get food and live. But a plant on the edge of a desert is said to struggle for life against the drought. . . . [S]everal seedling mistletoes, growing close together on the same branch, may . . . be said to struggle with each other. As the mistletoe is disseminated by birds, its existence depends on them; and it may methodically be said to struggle with other fruit-bearing plants, in tempting the birds to devour and thus disseminate its seeds. In these several senses, which pass into each other, I use for convenience' sake the general term of Struggle for Existence.

Darwin had to be careful not to depict nature as violent and brutal, or he would seem to challenge the contemporary Christian doctrine that nature had been created by a benevolent and wise God. The idea of all organisms constantly struggling against one another hardly supported the image of a loving Creator. Thus Darwin concluded the chapter with the following: "When we reflect on this struggle, we may console ourselves with the full belief, that the war of nature is not incessant, that no fear is felt, that death is generally prompt, and that the vigorous, the healthy, and the happy survive and multiply."

Chapter 4 introduced the concept of natural selection. Since variations occurred that humans have found useful in domesticated organisms, it should be reasonable

> that other variations useful in some way to each being in the great and complex battle of life, should occur in the course of many successive generations. If such do occur, can we doubt (remembering that many more individuals are born than can possibly survive) that individuals having any advantage, however slight, over others, would have the best chance of surviving and of procreating their kind? On the other hand, we may feel sure that any variation in the least degree injurious would be rigidly destroyed. This preservation of favourable individual differences and variations, and the destruction of those which are injurious, I have called Natural Selection, or the Survival of the Fittest. [Earlier, Darwin gives Herbert Spencer credit for the latter phrase.]

Darwin also discussed the principle of divergence here, showing how, over time, the descendants of one species will become specialized for different ways of life, resulting in new species. Chapter 4 contained the only illustration in the *Origin,* a branching diagram showing how natural selection leads to divergent evolution, creating new species. Significantly, the diagram had no central trunk. There is no great goal at the center of Darwin's evolutionary scheme. Many readers would have preferred for Darwin to propose that natural selection was directed toward the goal of creating humankind.

In chapter 5, "Laws of Variation," Charles struggled to explain how and why organisms vary and how those variations are passed on. However, as he admitted, "Our ignorance of the laws of variation is profound." Even so, he wrote, we see that variations occur and that they can be passed on. It wouldn't be until the early twentieth century and the understanding of basic genetics that this problem was solved.

The middle section of the book covered arguments and objections that Darwin thought would be made to his theory. He went on to describe how natural selection explained phenomena such as the apparent progress of species in the fossil record, the absence of mammals and frogs on oceanic islands, and the presence of partly formed organs with no apparent function, such as the human appendix.

The final chapter was an extensive summary. Darwin, ever nervous about the reception his ideas would get, did his best to avoid upsetting his readers. He wrote of the origin of life, "[A]ll the organic beings which have ever lived on this earth have descended from some one primordial form, into which life was first breathed." This statement left open divine creation of the first living thing. However, Darwin couldn't resist adding, when writing of future research, "Much light will be thrown on the origin of man and his history."

He concludes with an uplifting vision:

There is grandeur in this view of life, with its several powers, having been originally breathed by the Creator into a few forms or into one; and that, whilst this planet has gone cycling on according to the fixed law of gravity, from so simple a beginning endless forms most beautiful and most wonderful have been, and are being evolved.

CHAPTER FOURTEEN

The Reaction to Natural Selection

CHARLES AWAITED THE REACTION to his book at a spa in the isolated town of Ilkley. Both the weather and Charles's health were dreadful. Charles's concern about the reception the *Origin* would receive could only have made his health worse. As he wrote to Joseph Hooker: "I have been very bad lately; having an awful 'crisis' one leg swelled like elephantiasis—eyes almost closed up—covered with a rash and fiery Boils: but they tell me it [the treatment] will surely do me much good—it was like living in Hell."

Hooker had read much of the book in proofs and commented favorably, so Charles was confident of his reaction to the final version. But Charles was worried about Lyell's opinion, for his geological theories formed the foundation for much of Darwin's thesis, and Charles looked up to Lyell as his mentor. Lyell had gotten a set of proofs in September. His response on October 3 showed admiration: "It is a splendid case of close reasoning & long sustained argument throughout, . . ." but he couldn't bring himself to accept the logical consequences of natural selection.

Charles was concerned about Lyell's hesitation and wrote him a long letter. If Lyell responded directly to Charles, his reply has not been preserved. But Charles did get a letter from Hooker stating, "Lyell, with whom we are staying, is perfectly enchanted and is absolutely gloating over it." Charles didn't know it, but Hooker far overstated the case; Lyell had not withdrawn his objections.

Thomas Huxley's response after reading proofs soon followed. He wrote, "I do most heartily thank you for the great store of new views you have given me." But he was not wholly convinced by Charles and cited what he saw as serious problems with the book. However, he concluded:

I trust you will not allow yourself to be in any way disgusted or annoyed by the considerable abuse & misrepresentation which unless I greatly mistake is in store for you—Depend upon it you have earned the lasting gratitude of all thoughtful men—And as to the curs which will bark & yelp—you must recollect that some of your friends at any rate are endowed with an amount of combativeness which (though you have often & justly rebuked it) may stand you in good stead—

I am sharpening up my claws & beak in readiness.

Despite Huxley's reservations, Darwin was relieved. He wrote back:

I should have been more than contented with one quarter of what you have said. Exactly fifteen months ago, when I put pen to paper for this volume, I had awful misgivings, & thought perhaps I had deluded myself like so many have done; & I then fixed in my mind three judges, on whose decision I determined mentally to abide. The judges were Lyell, Hooker & yourself. . . .

Now Charles felt he could withstand the storm to follow. The three judges he had set for himself were, he believed, convinced of the truth of his ideas, and that mattered most.

Charles spent two days in London before returning home to Down from Ilkley and had a chance to test the reactions to his book. A long meeting with Richard Owen, the paleontologist who studied the fossils Charles brought from South America, proved very unpleasant. Owen was quite opposed to Charles's ideas. Owen was known as a difficult man, and evidence of his hostility toward Darwin showed up later in a very nasty review. The author was anonymous, but everyone knew Owen had written it.

Adam Sedgwick, ever an ardent opponent of evolution, responded to Charles's book with a very unkind letter on November 24: "I have read your book with more pain than pleasure. Parts of it I admired greatly; parts I

Richard Owen, a difficult man to get along with, who strongly opposed Darwin, shown in 1851

laughed at until my sides were almost sore; other parts I read with absolute sorrow; because I think them utterly false & grievously mischievous."

Charles wasn't surprised by Sedgwick's response, but he was still hurt.

In the 1860s, things happened more slowly than they do today. With no radio or television, no author book tours, and fewer educated people who could afford to buy books, new ideas took some time to catch on. Getting a hearing for natural selection would take effort, and the ideas expressed in the *Origin* needed to be promoted, defended, and explained. Charles lacked the combative spirit to defend his ideas publicly, but he had Huxley.

Thomas Huxley became known as "Darwin's Bulldog." He relished confrontation and realized that Charles's ideas could be used to bolster a liberal political agenda. The Anglican church and the aristocracy controlled English politics and society, and liberals like Huxley held a more egalitarian viewpoint. If nature rather than God was responsible for the living world, including humankind, the authority of the Anglican church would be seriously weakened.

Church and evolution clashed for the first time on June 30, 1860, at a meeting of the British Association for the Advancement of Science in Oxford.

With about seven hundred people in the audience, Samuel Wilberforce, Bishop of Oxford, launched an attack on evolution, Darwin, and his supporters. In conclusion, Wilberforce turned to Huxley and said: "I should like to ask Professor Huxley, who is sitting by me, and is about to tear me to pieces when I have sat down, as to his belief in being descended from an ape. Is it on his grandfather's or his grandmother's side that the ape ancestry comes in?"

The unruffled Huxley responded: "I should feel it no shame to have risen from such an origin. But I should feel it a shame to have sprung from one who prostituted the gifts of culture and of eloquence to the service of prejudice and falsehood."

Better an ape for an ancestor than a human like Wilberforce. Huxley continued with a defense of evolution and was followed by Hooker and another supporter. Wilberforce had been outclassed. The evolutionists had won this round, and the public battle had begun.

Bishop "Soapy Sam" Wilberforce in a caricature from Punch magazine, 1869

Wilberforce's wife had a more practical attitude than her husband. When she heard of the idea that humans had evolved, she responded, "Descended from the apes—my dear, let us hope that it is not true, but if it is, let us pray that it not become generally known."

Living at Down helped insulate Charles somewhat from the furor his book created. It was better for Darwin to read in the newspapers and letters about the debate than to be in the center of controversy in London. However, despite his relative isolation, he found himself devoting much of his time and energy to the *Origin* throughout the 1860s—revising it, writing letters to clear up misunderstandings about it, worrying about it. Altogether, the *Origin* would go through five revisions, each of which tried to counter new claims of critics. The final, sixth edition was published in February 1872.

Despite the constant challenges to his ideas and despite his frequent ill health, Darwin continued to study, experiment, and write about evolutionary topics. In 1862, his book *On the Various Contrivances by Which British and Foreign Orchids Are Fertilised by Insects* came out. It may seem strange that Charles chose to study a topic that seems so obscure. But Charles's interest lay in applying his theory to living things.

Beautiful flowers needed no explanation, people felt, and their loveliness spoke for God's glorious creation. But after careful study, Charles showed that every small variation in the structure of orchid flowers served to increase the chances that insects would take pollen from one blossom and carry it to

Darwin unraveled many secrets of orchids

another flower. Charles loved this kind of detective work. "You cannot conceive how the Orchids have delighted me," he wrote to Hooker, who supplied him with exotic specimens from Kew Gardens.

Through all this time, Charles kept believing his revered mentor, Lyell, would finally come out publicly for evolution in his book about the geological history of man. But the leap to accepting natural selection was too much for the older man. When Lyell's book *Antiquity of Man* was finally published in 1863, Charles opened it eagerly, only to be bitterly disappointed.

Charles wrote to Hooker: "The Lyells are coming here on Sunday evening to stay till Wednesday. I dread it, but I must say how much disappointed I am that he has not spoken out on species, still less on man. . . ."

Ultimately, Charles just could not face Lyell and became so ill he canceled the visit. It was easier to put his reaction into a letter to Lyell: "I will first get out what I hate saying, viz., that I have been greatly disappointed that you have not given judgment and spoken fairly out what you think about the derivation of species. . . ."

Lyell defended himself:

But you ought to be satisfied, as I shall bring hundreds towards you, who if I treated the matter more dogmatically would have rebelled.

I have spoken out to the utmost extent of my tether so far as my reason goes, and farther than my imagination and sentiment can follow. . . .

Meanwhile, the illness that made Charles cancel the Lyells' visit did not go away. Charles continued vomiting and suffered a bout of eczema. The eczema went away only to be replaced by terrible headaches. In September 1863, Emma finally got him to travel to Malvern, despite the sad memories of Annie's death. While there, they received a letter from a devastated Hooker telling them his own six-year-old daughter had just died. Hooker's news revived Charles and Emma's anguish over Annie's death. Charles became sicker and sicker. The couple returned to Down, where Charles became so weak he couldn't write; Emma had to take dictation. He only began to improve in the spring of 1864.

Once *The Origin of Species* was published, both science and society had to reconsider the concept of evolution. *Vestiges of Creation*, by then known to have been written by a publisher and amateur geologist named Robert

Chambers, had excited much interest, but Chambers hadn't proposed a mechanism for evolution. In the *Origin*, Charles had both advanced a mechanism and shown how it could explain so much in the natural world.

Darwin had also worked carefully behind the scenes to convince prominent scientists of his ideas before publishing. Not only Hooker and Huxley, but many other influential men, were already in Darwin's camp when the *Origin* was published.

Once an idea is out, no one can control what others do with it. So it was with Darwin's version of evolution. Darwin had finally broken the barrier, writing a book that made the idea of evolution ultimately acceptable to both science and society. His name became synonymous with evolution, but not necessarily evolution by natural selection.

Many men labeled as Darwinists during the late nineteenth century were actually pseudo-Darwinists. They favored evolution, but they added and subtracted freely from Darwin's theory. Since no one understood genetics, people could freely speculate about where variation came from and how it might be passed on from one generation to the next.

Liberal thinkers like Huxley, who wanted to change English society and to weaken the power of the Anglican church and the aristocracy, welcomed the *Origin*. The philosopher Herbert Spencer was an especially influential liberal thinker and writer who developed his own brand of evolution and originated the phrase "survival of the fittest." Under pure Darwinism, if an individual exhibited a harmful trait, it had no chance of surviving and reproducing. This idea bothered Spencer.

Spencer's evolutionary theory gave individuals a chance of bettering themselves. In Spencer's world, the environment and the organism interacted intimately in the process of evolution. This made evolution more palatable to the Victorians, who believed that individual effort should be rewarded. Spencer envisioned a progressive evolution that worked toward betterment. Evolution could then be seen to have purpose instead of being the mechanical process envisioned by Darwin.

While Darwin was not able to convince everyone that natural selection was the major driving force behind evolution, *The Origin of Species* did make science and society accept the mutability of species. Like Spencer, Christians who decided to accept evolution had a hard time with natural selection. Random variation included no divine element, and the concept of the strug-

Herbert Spencer, a philosopher who developed his own version of evolution, circa 1880

gle for existence seemed to promote selfishness. But Darwin's volume had demonstrated forcefully that evolution is adaptive, and this needed to be explained. In the end, conservative Christians like Owen ended up relying on the old Lamarckian ideas, such as the inheritance of acquired traits, just as Spencer did. But for them, evolution became the unfolding of a divine purpose leading to increasing perfection.

The novelist Samuel Butler became one of the most influential proponents of this new form of largely Lamarckian evolution. The inheritance of acquired characteristics, he claimed, explained evolution much better than natural selection. Natural selection left no place for the Creator. But if animals could actively choose new ways of doing things that were then passed on to their offspring, the Creator could be taking an active role. As historian of science Peter J. Bowler writes, in Butler's universe, "Instead of designing species from the outside, so to speak, God works through the purposeful behaviour of the animals to which He has delegated His creative power."

CHAPTER FIFTEEN

Darwin at Work

Although Darwin continued to correspond with his supporters and to revise the *Origin* up until 1872, he kept himself apart from the scientific and philosophical battles his book inspired. Illness took up much of his time, and when he felt well enough to work, he preferred to write new material and to carry out simple experiments, mostly with plants. By working at home, Charles was able to adjust his schedule to his unreliable health and to spend time with his family. If he could get in three good hours of work a day, he was happy.

As his health improved after his serious bout of illness from 1863 to 1864, Charles became intrigued by climbing plants. They crowded his study and greenhouse, and he asked Hooker for more specimens. He also worked on his book *The Variation of Plants and Animals under Domestication*. Charles remained convinced that details of the process of artificial selection bolstered his theory of natural selection.

By this time, Darwin's supporters dominated the prestigious Royal Society, and in November 1864, he was told he would receive the society's greatest honor, the Copley Medal. As had been true with the Royal Medal earlier, the congratulations of his friends and colleagues meant more to him than the award itself. He feared that traveling to London to receive the medal would harm his health, so he stayed home.

At a celebratory dinner after the ceremony, Lyell inched closer to accept-

Climbing plants, shown here in the Down greenhouse today, were one of Charles's delights

ing natural selection. As he wrote to Charles, he made a "confession of faith as to the Origin. . . . I said I had been forced to give up my old faith without thoroughly seeing my way to a new one. But I think you would have been satisfied with the length I went."

In April 1865, Charles's health once again collapsed. In September, he tried yet another doctor, who prescribed dieting and exercise. As Charles wrote to Hooker:

I am sure he had done me good by rigorous diet. I have been half-starved to death and am 15 lb lighter, but I have gained in walking power and my vomiting is immensely reduced. I have my hopes of again some day resuming scientific work, which is my sole enjoyment in life.

By April 1866, Charles was well enough to attend a Royal Society function. He had grown a beard, and many of his friends didn't recognize him. That year saw sad changes in Charles's personal life. In February, his younger sister Catherine died, followed by older sister Susan in October. The Mount, no longer a center for family gatherings, was put up for sale.

The Variation of Animals and Plants under Domestication went to the publisher in January 1867 and was issued the following January. Charles's health was better than it had been for a long time. He had begun horseback riding as part of his most recent recovery, and it continued to bring him enjoyment. "It does suit me admirably, and I am very much stronger," he wrote to Fox.

Meanwhile, the *Origin* had spread over to continental Europe and crossed the Atlantic to America. Darwin had become an international figure. While the book stimulated debate everywhere, it was especially well accepted in Germany. The French, however, did not think so highly of Darwin.

Charles's next project was to write about human origins. He had left mankind out of the *Origin* because he feared that the resulting controversy would overwhelm his theory of natural selection. By 1869, however, evolution had become well accepted, and several other scientists had already published works on evolution and man. In 1868, Charles sent letters to many specialists with knowledge of different animal groups to gather evidence for the book, which grew and grew until it finally became two volumes.

The Descent of Man actually covered two topics, human evolution and the role played by a process Darwin dubbed "sexual selection" in evolution. The two topics may seem distinct, but it was the study of human differences that led Charles to the concept of sexual selection. He believed that human racial differences arose because individuals chose their mates on the basis of different criteria. For example, if two groups of humans had different concepts of feminine beauty, the males would choose different-looking mates. Over time, as those "beautiful" traits were selected in the two societies, the people would come to look different. Traits such as the spectacular tail fan of the peacock, Darwin wrote, had also developed by sexual selection.

In February 1871, *The Descent of Man* was published. The scientific and public climate had changed dramatically over the twelve years since the first edition of *The Origin of Species.* Reviews of *Descent* were generally respectful, and many were favorable. Darwin's greatest challenge in *Descent* lay in

A cartoon showing an apelike Darwin, circa 1872

convincing readers that the human mind is not unique, that hints of the qualities associated with being human can be found in other animals. He presented many examples of animal intelligence.

He wrote that dogs can learn to understand what we say to them:

When I say to my terrier, in an eager voice (and I have made the trial many times), "Hi, hi, where is it?" she at once takes it as a sign that something is to be hunted, and generally first looks quickly all around, and then rushes into the nearest thicket, to scent for any game, but finding nothing, she looks up into any neighbouring tree for a squirrel. Now do not these actions clearly shew that she had in her mind a general idea or concept that some animal is to be discovered and hunted?

Monkeys can learn, he pointed out:

Rengger, a most careful observer, states that when he first gave eggs to his monkeys in Paraguay, they smashed them, and thus lost much of their contents; afterwards they gently hit one end against some hard body, and picked off the bits of shell with their fingers. After cutting themselves only once with any sharp tool, they would not touch it again, or would handle it with the greatest caution.

Darwin's next task was to link humans to other animals by showing similarities in expression of emotions. Charles had been interested in this topic for decades and had been making notes about it since 1837. His interest in emotional expression and development had been spurred while he was writing down his observations of baby William in 1839. Charles collected countless photos of both humans and animals to study facial expressions and gestures.

Punch cartoon making fun of Charles's work on human emotions, circa 1872

He wrote to anthropologists asking such questions as, Do the people you study show anger, surprise, and other emotions in the same way Europeans do? He queried mental hospitals asking if the expressions of the inmates were identical to those of mentally healthy people. He visited the London zoo to study monkeys and apes and drew upon his lifelong experiences with dogs. Backed by the impressive array of facts he gathered, Darwin showed that people of different ages, cultures, and mental health all have similar facial expressions and that these expressions are often like those of certain animals.

The Expression of the Emotions in Man and Animals received mixed but mostly favorable reviews. Wallace wrote in the *Quarterly Journal of Science* about Darwin's "insatiable longing to discover the causes of the varied and complex phenomena presented by living things" and commented on Charles's intense childlike curiosity.

Charles himself, however, felt spent by his efforts. As he wrote to Ernst Haeckel, a German colleague: "I have resumed some old botanical work, and perhaps I shall never again attempt to discuss theoretical views. I am growing old and weak, and no man can tell when his intellectual powers begin to fail."

Most sixty-three-year-olds would be satisfied to relax after a distinguished career that brought the highest honors a country can give. But not Charles. His son Francis helped in his continuing research. During the last decade of his life, Charles wrote five more books, seven revised editions of previous books, and produced almost three dozen scientific papers.

The devoted Emma watched carefully over Charles, making sure the couple got away from Down House and Charles's work on a regular basis. Charles knew these breaks were good for him, but he didn't necessarily enjoy them. As he wrote to Huxley in October 1872: "We return home Saturday after three weeks of the most astounding dullness, doing nothing and thinking of nothing. . . . I hope my Brain likes it—for myself it is dreadful doing nothing."

With his children grown and his legacy established, Charles's health improved. He enjoyed his life more than he had for a long time. During the 1870s, three of his children married, and one grandson was born. Even after marriage, however, his children and their families loved coming to Down House.

Charles continued to be a loyal friend, too. In 1879 he proposed that Alfred Wallace, who had done so much important scientific work, be provided with a government pension. Many colleagues agreed, and the government acquiesced. "Good Heavens! how pleased I am," Charles wrote to Hooker.

In August 1881, Charles's beloved brother, Erasmus, died after a short illness. Erasmus had never married, and he left his fortune to Charles. When added to the inheritance the family would receive from an admirer named Anthony Rich, the Darwin clan was assured financial security. Charles decided to spend part of his wealth on the advancement of science. He arranged for Kew Gardens to undertake a complete index of all the plants that had been described, including all the synonyms that had confused scientists. He also bequeathed money to foster research in geology and zoology.

Darwin's last book, *The Formation of Vegetable Mould, through the Action of Worms, with Observations on Their Habits,* came out in October 1881. Because it could easily be understood and because it dealt with familiar creatures, it became one of his most popular volumes.

On December 11, 1881, Charles suffered a heart attack while traveling. Back at Down House, he continued to be ill, with frequent and painful angina and further attacks. April 18, 1882, brought a severe attack, and Darwin died the following day.

Charles had wanted to be buried in the Down churchyard next to his brother Erasmus and his dead infant children. His family and the people of the village also wanted him there.

Charles used this "worm stone" in the garden at Down to measure the activities of earthworms

Some of Darwin's colleagues, however, had other ideas. They thought that since Darwin was among England's greatest men, he deserved to join the best in Westminster Abbey, the great official church in London. After all, Charles had expressed delight when Lyell had been buried there in 1875. After much political scheming, the church agreed. Pressure on the family finally made them go along with the plan.

On April 26, 1882, Charles Darwin was laid to rest in Westminster Abbey, the burial place of kings and saints, near other great scientists such as Isaac Newton. Emma stayed home at Down House, where she felt much closer to him than she could have amidst the pomp and ceremony Charles himself would clearly have abhorred.

CHAPTER SIXTEEN

Darwin's Legacy

THE EVOLUTIONARY BIOLOGIST ERNST MAYR sums up Charles Darwin's genius best: "A brilliant mind, great intellectual boldness, and an ability to combine the best qualities of a naturalist-observer, philosophical theoretician, and experimentalist—the world has so far seen such a combination only once, and it was in the man Charles Darwin."

In recent years, interest in this great man has grown, for many reasons. Publication of *The Correspondence of Charles Darwin* by Cambridge University Press has provided scholars around the world with easy access to original material. Darwin's letters to family, friends, and colleagues reveal much about his character, emotions, and thought. As more volumes are issued, even more will be learned about how Darwin worked and reasoned. Many of Darwin's notebooks have also been published word for word, so historians of science can follow the development of his many groundbreaking concepts about the natural world.

Study of these documents has cleared up some important misconceptions about Darwin that unfortunately still appear in some textbooks. He was not an aimless young man who wasn't interested in learning and who was rescued from obscurity by the opportunity to travel on the *Beagle.* He didn't suddenly discover natural selection while in the Galapagos Islands, nor was his reluctance to publish based purely on fear of disapproval. The more we learn about Darwin, the more complex and the more revolutionary he becomes.

Charles in 1880, two years before his death

Much of Darwin's genius lay in his faith in his own ability to observe the world accurately and to trust his own observations instead of blindly believing what others told him. When he was young, he believed Anglican doctrine; he had no reason to doubt it. But as he traveled on the *Beagle,* he saw things that contradicted the concept of a loving God who had made a perfect world for the use of humankind. The evils of slavery he reacted to so intensely in South America made no sense if God were loving, and the viciousness he observed of slave owners provided evidence that humans did not necessarily behave like divinely created, superior beings. The Fuegians seemed to Charles more different from "civilized" people than wild animals were from domesticated ones, impressing upon him how close humans really are to other animals.

Charles's observations of the natural world also contradicted church dogma. If God created all species as perfect, why did any become extinct? And if they were perfect, why did individual plants and animals succumb to drought, disease, predation, and other perils of existence? The vast number of

PUNCH'S ALMANACK FOR 1882.

MAN · IS · BVT · A · WORM.

Punch's version of evolution, starting with a worm at the bottom and ending up with Darwin

diverse life-forms in the tropics also strained the credulity of the concept that God created such species individually.

Once Darwin conceived of evolution by natural selection, all his observations fell into place in a scheme that made sense. He realized he had found the answer, and he had no problem discarding the dogma that made no sense. As he wrote in his autobiography:

> As far as I can judge, I am not apt to follow blindly the lead of other men. I have steadily endeavoured to keep my mind free, so as to give up any hypothesis, however much beloved (and I cannot resist forming one on every subject), as soon as facts are shown to be opposed to it.

Darwin's ability to focus on his observations and to base his thinking on them allowed him to develop a viable theory of evolution even though genetics was not yet understood. Darwin's theory brings together three necessary elements—random variation in organisms, the struggle for existence, and the principle of divergence—to create a coherent theory that makes sense of biology, of what we observe in the natural world.

After biologists learned early in the twentieth century that traits are dictated by genes that lie on chromosomes in the nucleus of each cell, natural selection made even more sense. Mutations of genes became recognized as the source of the variations that fuel natural selection. Modern genetics also shows that Darwin was mistaken in his belief that the inheritance of acquired characteristics played a small part in evolution. But without an understanding of genetics, there was no firm reason to reject this idea.

We have also learned that factors other than natural selection can play a role in evolution. Several times in the history of life on Earth, major catastro-

Darwin's study right after his death

phes have killed off the vast majority of living things. How well species were adapted to their environments meant little or nothing when the impact of a meteor, for example, abolished entire ecosystems and shot so much dust into the atmosphere that plants could barely photosynthesize. Under such circumstances, chance probably played a significant role in which organisms died out and which survived. But once the catastrophe was over, natural selection worked on the survivors to produce the organisms that would live in the new, changed world.

The more we learn, the more we realize how complex the evolutionary history of Earth has been. However, whatever additional facts we discover, natural selection still remains at the core of evolution. The simplicity of this powerful force is amazing: if an organism can survive to reproduce, it can pass its genes on to the next generation. That is the fundamental mechanism of evolution.

As Jonathan Weiner pointed out in *The Beak of the Finch,* his book about the outstanding work of Peter and Rosemary Grant on speciation of Darwin's finches in the Galapagos Islands, "the *Origin* does not document the origin of a single species, or a single case of natural selection, or the preservation of one favored race in the struggle for life."

The theory Darwin presented in *The Origin of Species* is based on observation, not experimentation. People have criticized it for this reason, but observation has always been a perfectly valid scientific tool, and it was the only tool available to Darwin for studying evolution.

Evolution often takes place over long periods of time, making it difficult to document precisely. Sometimes, however, we can follow its course. One early evolutionary study showed how the predominant form of the peppered moth in Great Britain changed from light to dark color after the Industrial Revolution blackened tree trunks in the countryside. In Manchester, for example, only one dark moth was caught in 1848, but by 1895 about 98 percent of the population of that heavily industrial region was dark. Before the Industrial Revolution, light moths were camouflaged against the light-colored lichen that covered tree trunks, so birds had a hard time seeing them. Afterward, however, the light moths were easy to pick off, and the dark ones survived to reproduce.

In the later part of the twentieth century, more field researchers have been able to study in detail how natural selection actually works in nature. Such study is difficult, for it requires many years of gathering an enormous quantity of data that must be analyzed. Before computers, this sort of research was virtually impossible. Now scientists can enter their data into a computer, tell the computer what to look for, and pinpoint important correlations in moments.

Peter and Rosemary Grant and their students have been studying Darwin's finches since 1973. They chose these birds because the environment in which they live is relatively simple. Most of the Grants' work has taken place on a small island in the Galapagos called Daphne Major. Few birds and few species of plants live there, so it is possible for the researchers to keep track of individual birds and what they eat. The birds are also quite easy to catch and then measure.

The Grants' results and those of other researchers show where Darwin was right and where he was wrong. Darwin would have expected a small population on a small island not to vary much. Instead, the finches on Daphne Major show amazing variability in everything from wing length to beak size. Darwin believed that natural selection worked slowly over long periods of time, like Lyell's geological processes. But the finch populations react quickly to environmental challenges such as drought or abundant rainfall. Within a generation, the balance on the island can tip strongly toward one species or another, depending on what kinds of seeds are most abundant.

Studies like that of the Grants also indicate that the unrelenting "struggle for existence" goes on every moment of every day. Evolution is a dynamic, ongoing process that can have significant effects in a short time, and natural selection can operate on a level of very fine detail. A millimeter or two difference in the size of a Galapagos finch's beak, for example, can mean the difference between life and death, between successful reproduction and failure to reproduce.

The work of other scientists has also documented the importance of natural selection. John Endler has studied the colors of wild guppies in South American streams. Male guppies attract mates by their brightly colored spots. But the spots can also make the fish more visible to predators. Endler found that the spots of the males are bigger and brighter where predators are few. In areas with lots of predators, the spots are smaller and fainter. The spots are an advantage to successful reproduction, if the male can survive long enough to reproduce. Natural selection acts constantly on the different guppy populations to favor bright males where predators are unlikely to eat them and duller males where they could be picked off before having a chance to mate.

Charles Darwin so changed how we see the world and how biological scientists carry out their work that it is difficult to evaluate his influence. While evolution by natural selection is his greatest legacy, Darwin pioneered many other fields of study. Before Darwin, most naturalists merely described what they found. Darwin wanted to understand the functions of the things he observed, so he combined his great powers of observation with simple experimental techniques he could use in his home study, garden, and greenhouse. His work on the classification of barnacles became a model for how to classify living things of any kind. Before Darwin, people simply marveled at phenomena such as the beauty of flowers and the ability of some plants to twine their way upward. Darwin looked deeper, into biological functions and mechanisms, to uncover the role of structure in how plants survive and reproduce. He helped teach biologists to ask, Why is that so? This is perhaps his greatest legacy.

# CHRONOLOGY

January 3, 1765: Charles's mother, Susannah Wedgwood, born

May 30, 1766: Charles's father, Robert Waring Darwin, born

May 2, 1808: Emma Wedgwood, Charles's cousin and future wife, born

February 12, 1809: Charles Darwin born in Shrewsbury

1812: War between U.S. and Britain; Napoleon invades Russia

1815: Napoleon defeated at Waterloo

Spring 1817: Charles and sister Catherine begin Mr. Case's school

July 15, 1817: Charles's mother dies

1818: Charles starts studying and living at Shrewsbury School

1820: First photograph

1825: First passenger railway in Britain

October 22, 1825: Charles enters Edinburgh University

January 1827: Charles enters Cambridge University

April 26, 1831: Charles receives BA degree from Cambridge

August 26, 1831: Charles is invited to join the *Beagle* voyage

September 1, 1831: Charles accepts invitation

December 27, 1831: The *Beagle* sails for South America

February 28, 1832: The *Beagle* lands at Bahia, first stop in South America

August 29–September 6, 1832: Charles collects important fossils at Punta Alta

December 16, 1832: The *Beagle* reaches Tierra del Fuego

March 10, 1835: Charles receives letter in the Falkland Islands from Henslow approving of his collecting

August 14–27, 1834: Charles makes a geological excursion to the base of the Andes mountains

February 20, 1835: Charles experiences a violent earthquake and observes the geological results

September 15–October 20, 1835: The *Beagle* explores the Galapagos Islands

April 1–12, 1836: The *Beagle* visits the Cocos-Keeling Islands

October 2, 1836: The *Beagle* returns to England

October 5, 1836: Charles returns to Shrewsbury after an absence of 5 years and 2 days

November 1836: Charles is elected a member of the Geological Society of London

December 16, 1836–March 6, 1837: Charles lives in Cambridge while working on his specimens from the *Beagle* voyage

1837: Queen Victoria ascends the throne

1837: Telegraph patented

March 6, 1837: Charles moves to London

September 28, 1838: Charles begins to read Malthus on population

January 24, 1839: Charles is elected a fellow of the Royal Society of London

January 29, 1839: Charles marries Emma Wedgwood

June 1, 1839: The *Journal of Researches,* Charles's book about the *Beagle* voyage, is published

December 27, 1839: The Darwin's first child, William, is born

1840: Penny-post introduced

August 4, 1840: Charles becomes so sick he stops writing letters for five months

March 2, 1841: Annie Darwin born

June 1842: Charles writes the first outline, which he termed a "pencil sketch," of his species theory

September 17, 1842: The Darwin family moves to Down House

September 23, 1842: Mary Darwin born, dies in October

1843: First steamship crosses the Atlantic

September 25, 1843: Henrietta Darwin born

January 11, 1844: Charles writes J. D. Hooker, "confessing" that he is an evolutionist

October 14, 1844: Charles writes to Leonard Jenyns of his evolutionary views

July 9, 1845: George Darwin born

August 26, 1845: Charles finishes the second edition of the *Journal of Researches*

1846: Ether first used as a surgical anesthetic

October 1846: Charles begins his barnacle work

July 8, 1847: Elizabeth Darwin born

July 1848–January 1849: Charles very ill for six months

August 16, 1848: Francis Darwin born

November 13, 1848: Charles's father dies

March 10–June 30, 1849: Charles receives hydropathic treatment at Malvern

January 15, 1850: Leonard Darwin born

April 23, 1851: Annie Darwin dies

May 13, 1851: Horace Darwin born

1852: Napoleon III becomes emperor of France

September 9, 1854: Charles begins sorting the notes for his book on species

March and April 1855: Charles begins experimenting on effects of salt on seeds

April 1856: Charles discusses Wallace's 1855 paper with Lyell; Lyell urges Charles to publish something about his ideas

May 14, 1856: Charles begins writing on natural selection for publication

July 20, 1856: Charles writes to Asa Gray and tells him about his evolutionary views

December 5, 1856: Charles Waring Darwin, Emma's last baby, is born

June 18, 1858: Wallace's manuscript, describing his version of natural selection, arrives; Charles writes immediately to Lyell

July 1, 1858: The joint paper describing Darwin's and Wallace's work is read to the Linnaean Society

July 20, 1858: Charles begins to write the "abstract" of his work that will become *The Origin of Species*

July 28, 1858: Infant son Charles Waring Darwin dies

March 19, 1859: Charles finishes *The Origin of Species*

November 24, 1858: *Origin* published

June 30, 1860: Hooker and Huxley debate with Wilberforce at Oxford

1861: U.S. Civil War begins

1863: Emancipation proclamation abolishes slavery in the U.S.

1863: First underground railway opens in London

November 30, 1864: Charles is awarded the Copley Medal by the Royal Society

1865: Joseph Lister introduces antiseptic surgery

April 28, 1865: FitzRoy commits suicide

February, 1866: Charles's sister Catherine Darwin dies

October 3, 1866: Charles's sister Susan Darwin dies

1867: First practical typewriter devised

January 30, 1868: Charles's book *The Variation of Animals and Plants under Domestication* is published

February 24, 1871: *The Descent of Man* is published

November 26, 1872: *The Expression of the Emotions in Man and Animals* is published

February 22, 1875: Sir Charles Lyell dies

July 2, 1875: *Insectivorous Plants* is published

September or November 1875: *Climbing Plants* is published

1876: Alexander Graham Bell invents the telephone

1879: Thomas Alva Edison makes the first lightbulb

August 26, 1881: Charles's brother Erasmus dies

October 10, 1881: Charles's last book, *The Formation of Vegetable Mould, through the Action of Worms, with Observations on Their Habits,* is published

April 19, 1882: Charles dies

April 26, 1882: Charles's funeral at Westminster Abbey is held

October 2, 1896: Emma Darwin dies

The Journey of the BEAGLE

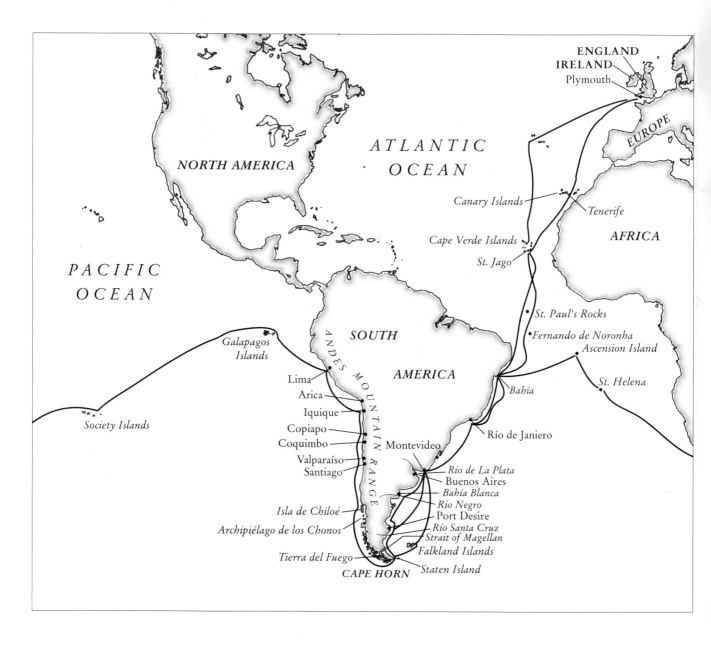

NORTH AMERICA

ATLANTIC
OCEAN

PACIFIC
OCEAN

ENGLAND
IRELAND
Plymouth

EUROPE

Canary Islands

Tenerife

AFRICA

Cape Verde Islands

St. Jago

St. Paul's Rocks

Fernando de Noronha
Ascension Island

Galapagos
Islands

SOUTH

AMERICA

St. Helena

Lima

ANDES MOUNTAIN RANGE

Arica

Iquique

Bahía

Copiapo

Coquimbo

Montevideo

Río de Janiero

Society Islands

Valparaíso
Santiago

Río de La Plata
Buenos Aires
Bahía Blanca
Río Negro
Port Desire
Río Santa Cruz
Strait of Magellan
Falkland Islands
Staten Island

Isla de Chiloé

Archipiélago de los Chonos

Tierra del Fuego

CAPE HORN

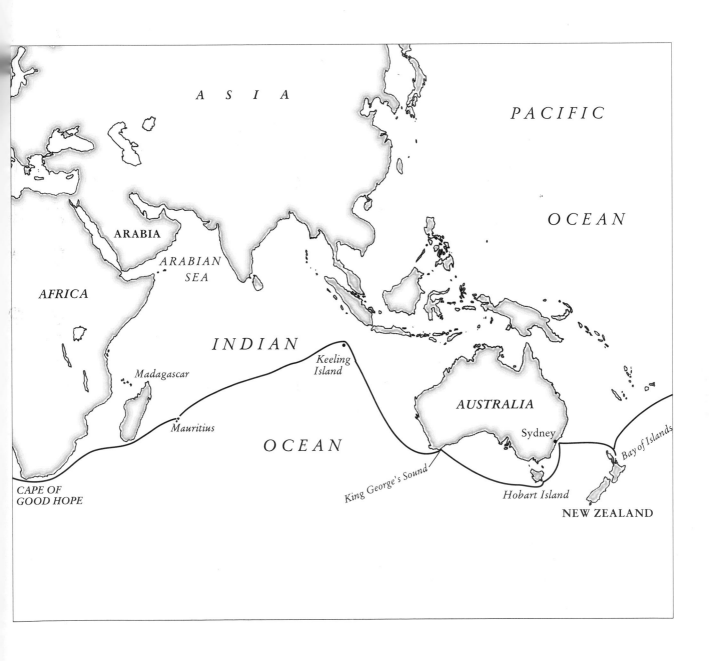

FRIENDS AND COLLEAGUES OF CHARLES DARWIN

Covington, Syms (1816–61): A sailor on the *Beagle* who became Darwin's servant on the voyage, then his secretary and scientific assistant until Covington emigrated to Australia in 1839.

Gould, John (1804–81): An ornithologist and artist who examined the birds Darwin collected in the Galapagos Islands and who described the all-important finches and mockingbirds. Gould also produced a much-admired set of color lithographs of birds and mammals.

Grant, Robert (1793–1874): A Scottish zoologist who befriended Charles in Edinburgh and introduced him to the scientific study of invertebrate animals. Later, he became a professor at University College in London.

Gray, Asa (1810–88): An American botanist and professor at Harvard University who was very interested in the species question. He became a friend and supporter of Charles and his theories.

Henslow, John Stevens (1796–1861): Professor of mineralogy and botany at Cambridge University, he was Charles's mentor and gave him the only scientific training he received at Cambridge. He recommended Charles for the *Beagle* voyage.

Hooker, Joseph Dalton (1817–1911): A botanist who became good friends with Charles and helped obtain specimens for him. Hooker became director of Kew Gardens after his father, William Hooker, died.

Humboldt, Alexander von (1769–1859): An adventurous and innovative scientist whose writings on his journey to South America inspired Charles to explore the tropics. He studied many natural phenomena, including the origin of tropical storms and the relationship between plants and their geographical environment. The major ocean current off South America, now called the Peru current, used to be named after him.

Huxley, Thomas Henry (1825–95): The English educator, comparative anatomist, and paleontologist who became Charles's most vocal defender. He was the grandfather of author Aldous Huxley, who wrote the famous novel *Brave New World.*

Jenyns, Leonard (1800–93): Naturalist and later clergyman who collected beetles with Charles at Cambridge. He catalogued the fish from the *Beagle* expedition for Charles.

Lyell, Charles (1797–1875): A brilliant geologist whose work proved that the Earth was ancient and that living things had existed for millions of years. Lyell gave us the names *Eocene, Miocene,* and *Pliocene* for the epochs of the Tertiary geological period. Lyell's work influenced Darwin profoundly, and the men became friends as well as colleagues.

Owen, Richard (1804–92): The paleontologist who examined the fossil mammal specimens Charles sent to England from South America. Later in Charles's career, Owen was a severe critic of Charles's ideas. Owen was a friend of Queen Victoria and founded the British Museum of Natural History. He recognized dinosaurs as a distinct group and named them.

Sedgwick, Adam (1785–1873): A Cambridge geology professor who taught Charles about fossils and how to carry out geological fieldwork. Sedgwick later became a critic of Charles's evolutionary theories.

Spencer, Herbert (1820–1903): A philosopher whose theories included evolutionary ideas. His many books helped bring the theory of evolution within the grasp of the general reading public. He also helped to establish sociology as an accepted discipline.

Wallace, Alfred Russel (1823–1913): Brilliant naturalist, explorer, and collector who came up with the idea of evolution by natural selection independently of Darwin in 1858. Wallace systematized the field of biogeography. His name is perpetuated in Wallace's line, a hypothetical boundary separating the two quite-distinct groups of plants and animals found in the Oriental and Australian biogeographic regions.

Wilberforce, Samuel (1805–73): Bishop of Oxford and well-known orator, nicknamed "Soapy Sam," who became one of Darwin's most vehement critics.

# GLOSSARY

extinct: No longer living or in existence.

fossil: The preserved remains or traces of living things of the past, such as hardened bones or imprints of plant leaves or footprints.

genetics: The study of inheritance, or how traits are passed from one generation of living things to the next.

immutability of species: The concept that God created species in their final form and that they cannot change.

invertebrates: Animals without backbones, such as snails, worms, insects, and sea stars.

natural selection: The idea that living things that are best adapted to their environment are most likely to survive to reproduce and pass on their traits to the next generation.

species: a group of related organisms that are capable of interbreeding with one another. Under natural conditions, the members of one species do not normally interbreed with other species to produce fertile offspring, although there are a few exceptions.

transmutation: The term used in Darwin's time for changes in species.

vertebrates: Animals with backbones, such as fish, frogs, lizards, dogs, and people.

SELECTED BIBLIOGRAPHY

In the text, all quotations for which no source is given come from Darwin's autobiography. Most of the remaining quotes are from *The Correspondence of Charles Darwin*, the compilation of letters to and from Darwin, as well as some other letters relating directly to his work, that is being made from the collection in the Darwin Archives at Cambridge University. I have kept the nonstandard punctuation and spelling used by Darwin and others in the quotations.

"Finch DNA Shows Darwin was Right." *The New York Times.* May 11, 1999.

Bowlby, John. *Charles Darwin: A New Life.* New York: W.W. Norton & Company, Inc., 1990.

Bowler, Peter J. *Charles Darwin: The Man and His Influence.* Cambridge, England: Cambridge University Press, 1996.

Browne, Janet. *Charles Darwin Voyaging.* Princeton, NJ: Princeton University Press, 1995.

Burkhardt, F. H., S. Smith, et al., eds. *The Correspondence of Charles Darwin.* Vols. 1–10 (1821–1862). Cambridge, England: Cambridge University Press, 1983–1996.

Burkhardt, Frederick, ed. *Charles Darwin's Letters: A Selection 1825–1859.* Cambridge, England: Cambridge University Press, 1996.

Chandos, John. *Boys Together: English Public Schools 1800–1864.* New Haven, CT: Yale University Press, 1984.

Darwin, Charles. *Charles Darwin's Diary of the Voyage of H.M.S. "Beagle."* Edited by Nora Barlow. Cambridge, England: Cambridge University Press, 1933.

——. *The Autobiography of Charles Darwin, 1809–1882.* Edited by Nora Barlow. New York: W.W. Norton & Company, Inc., 1958.

——. *The Origin of Species, with a special introduction by Julian Huxley.* New York: New American Library, Inc., 1958.

——. *Charles Darwin's Notebooks, 1836–1844.* Edited by Paul H. Barrett et al. Ithaca, New York: Cornell University Press, 1987.

——. *Voyage of the Beagle: Charles Darwin's Journal of Researches.* Edited by Janet Browne and Michael Neve. New York: Penguin Books, 1989.

——. *Journal of Researches into the Natural History and Geology of the Countries Visited during the Voyage of the H.M.S. Beagle Round the World.* London: T. Nelson and Sons, 1890.

Darwin, Francis. *The Life of Charles Darwin.* Twickenham, England: Senate, 1995.

Goldie, Pete, creator. *Darwin 2nd Edition Multimedia CD-ROM.* San Francisco: Lightbinders, Inc, 1997.

Gribbin, John, and Michael White. *Darwin: A Life in Science.* New York: Dutton, 1995.

Huggett, Frank E. *How It Happened.* Oxford: Basil Blackwell & Mott Limited, 1971.

King-Hele, Desmond. *Erasmus Darwin: Grandfather of Charles Darwin.* New York: Charles Scribner's Sons, 1963.

Kohn, D., ed. *The Darwinian Heritage.* Princeton, NJ: Princeton University Press, 1985.

Marsden, Gordon, ed. *Victorian Values: Personalities and Perspectives in Nineteenth Century Society.* Essex, England: Longman Group UK Limited, 1990.

Mellersh, H.E.L. *FitzRoy of the Beagle.* N. p.: Mason & Lipscomb, 1968.

Moore, James, and Adrian Desmond. *Darwin: The Life of a Tormented Evolutionist.* New York: W.W. Norton & Company, Inc., 1991.

Overy, Caroline. *A Teacher's Guide to Charles Darwin, His Life, Journeys and Discoveries.* London: English Heritage, 1997.

Pool, Daniel. *What Jane Austen Ate and Charles Dickens Knew: Fascinating Facts of Daily Life in the Nineteenth Century.* London: Robinson Publishing Ltd, 1998.

Raverat, Gwen. *Period Piece: A Cambridge Childhood.* London: Faber and Faber Limited, 1952.

Sheets-Johnstone, Maxine. "Why Lamarck Did Not Discover the Principle of Natural Selection." *Journal of Historical Biology* 15, no. 3 (fall 1882): 443–465.

Stanbury, David, ed. *A Narrative of the Voyage of the H.M.S. Beagle,* Chatham, England: The Folio Society, W & J Mackay Limited, 1977.

Sulloway, Frank J. "Darwin and His Finches: The Evolution of a Legend." *Journal of the History of Biology* 15, no. 1 (spring 1982): 1–53.

——. "Darwin's Conversion: The Beagle Voyage and its Aftermath." *Journal of the History of Biology* 15, no. 3 (fall 1982): 325–396.

——. "The Beagle Collections of Darwin's Finches (Geospizinae)." *Bulletin of the British Museum of Natural History (Zoology)* 43, no. 2 (30 September 1982): 49–94.

———. "Darwin and the Galapagos." *Biological Journal of the Linnean Society* 21 (1984): 29–59.

Thomson, Keith S. *HMS Beagle: The Story of Darwin's Ship.* New York: W.W. Norton & Company, Inc., 1995.

Weiner, Jonathan. *The Beak of the Finch: A Story of Evolution in Our Time.* New York: Alfred A. Knopf, 1994.

Wilson, Louise and Solene Morris. *Down House: The Home of Charles Darwin.* London: English Heritage, 1998.

INTERNET RESOURCES

On Darwin's works:
Darwin's major works online: www.literature.org/authors/darwin-charles/
The Darwin-Wallace 1858 Evolution Paper online:
www.inform.umd.edu/PBIO/darwin/darwindex.html

On the *Beagle*:
An annotated map of the voyage: www.ucr.edu/h-gig/maps/beagle1.html
The journal of Syms Covington, Darwin's assistant on the voyage:
www.asap.unimelb.edu.au/bsparcs/covingto/

On the Galapagos Islands:
The Charles Darwin Foundation: www.darwinfoundation.org
The Galapagos Conservation Trust: www.gct.org/index.html

On Evolution:
Harvard University's biology links on evolution:
mcb.harvard.edu/BioLinks/Evolution.html
The National Center for Science Education's links on evolution:
www.natcenscied.org/link.asp?category=1
The University of California at Berkeley Museum of Paleontology's resources, lessons, and information on evolution:
www.ucmp.berkeley.edu/museum/k-12.html
The American Museum of Natural History's online exhibit on fossils:
www.amnh.org/Exhibition/Expediton/Fossils/fossils.frames.index.html
A companion website to the Public Broadcasting Corporation's Nature *series on evolution:* www.pbs.org/wnet/nature/triumphoflife/
The British Broadcasting Corporation's educational website on evolution:
www.bbc.co.uk/education/darwin/index.shtml

INDEX

(Page numbers in *italic* refer to illustrations.)